TWIN IN A COFFIN

by
Dean Ekaragha

The characters in this book are entirely fictional. Any resemblance to actual persons living or dead is entirely coincidental.

ISBN: 9798810664383
Imprint: Independently published

Chapter 1

April

"PLEASE! PLEASE! PLEASE!!" April cried out. Her 4-year old body cringing and shaking as she hysterically cried and begged for her kidnapper Shereece to take her home. "Please take me home, I want my mummy."

Shereece sat there on top of a dark brown wooden coffin, in a wide spider web infested basement that harboured several other coffins. Shereece stared right into innocent April's 4 year-old face with a bewildered expression. A dimly lit light bulb provided enough light for April and Shereece to see each other.

"You said you loved me," Shereece said to April. "You said you loved me April, and I love you too. I'll be your mummy from now on baby. I'll be the best mummy in the world to you, better than your other mother. She's a bad woman and a bad mother. I'm much better than her. I'll take care of you April, we already spoke about this," Shereece said, desperately trying to win April over.

"You said you want to be with me. This is your home now baby. Here, look at the present I got for you today." Shereece reached into her black leather bag lying beside her leg. She then withdrew a small brown teddy bear and handed it to April.

"No!" April screamed, whacking the teddy bear out of Shereece's hand. "I want to go home! Take me home to my mummy, my real mummy. You're not my mummy." Shereece slowly took her eyes off April and began to weep.

The infant and Shereece were now both crying, then suddenly Shereece's weeping turned into rage. With clenched fists and gritted teeth, Shereece abruptly stood up from the coffin she was sitting on and began to pace up and down the basement breathing heavily.

Her plan was not going according to what her demented mind made her believe would happen. There was now a massive police search for April whom Shereece had been holding captive for two days.

April was one of the infants that Shereece had looked after in the nursery where she worked, and she had grown excessively fond of Shereece over the past 12 months. Shereece had also fallen in love with the little girl and had long obsessed over having April as her own.

Shereece could not biologically have children and she desired nothing more than to raise the cute little girl as her own. However, as much as April was fond of Shereece, being kept hidden away and not seeing her parents became too much for April to bear.

Realising that she had been deluded, Shereece now began to feel hate towards the little girl she had once loved and dark sinister thoughts came to her mind.
Heartbroken and angry, Shereece turned to April and began punching and pounding her massive fists and arms against April's small body and head with all of her might, WHAM! WHAM! WHAM!

April tried to scream but couldn't get her voice out because of the repetitive blows to the head she was enduring. Shereece was a prolific weight lifter and her arms were broad and muscular. April was seconds away from losing consciousness.

Stopping her rain of blows, Shereece picked up April and with all her strength slammed her head into the concrete wall cracking April's skull, instantly killing her.

Chapter 2

Derrick & Kia

"You really don't have to come Derrick, it's totally fine. I'll probably stay just for the weekend and be back by Monday," Kia said to Derrick.

"No Kia I'm coming," Derrick replied firmly. "I want to come. I want to meet her; I mean we've been married for 2 years and I've never actually met your Twiiiinnn sister," Derrick said, stretching out the word twin. "Do you realise how odd that is Kia? Besides, you said yourself she insisted you bring me along with you. She wants to meet me."

"Derrick we've gone through this before. You know I don't really like talking about my family," Kia protested standing across the open plan living room/ kitchen. Derrick was sitting on the floor in his boxers with the back of his head leaning on the sofa.

"Before we got married what did you tell me Kia? You told me there would be no secrets between us, is that not what you said?"

"Yes Derrick, I know but-" Derrick hastily cut off his wife before she could finish her sentence, "But nothing Kia. I mean as much as I love you, you not opening up to me about your family makes me feel like there is this wall between us, and I don't want to have that feeling babes.

All you've ever told me about your sister is that she's weird. I'd love to meet her.

And now she's recently had a miscarriage and found out she can't have kids, JESUS!" he exclaimed, "that's a lot on her.

Sounds to me like she's going to need quite a bit of support. I'm a doctor Kia, I've dealt with patients that have had miscarriages many times and believe me the more support and love they receive at times like this, the better," Derrick said to his wife, now getting up off the floor and walking slowly towards Kia.

Kia was a five-foot four beauty of mixed race with a beautiful body. She had long wavy hair extensions. She was yoga slim, not skinny but fit slim. She scheduled 4 visits to the gym each week and never missed a session. She had opened up two hair & beauty salons in Essex where she now lived and business was good with the money flowing in from both salons. To top it off, she fell in love and married Derrick who was now a successful doctor.

Derrick was a six-foot tall black, athletically built, handsome man. He had a well-groomed beard and kept a low-cut hair shape up.

Everyone always said he resembled the actor Morris Chestnut. At the age of thirty, it was fair to say Kia and Derrick were a successful couple.

Derrick walked up to Kia and held the bottom of her chin, drawing her face to his before giving her a soft, passionate kiss. He then slowly rubbed his right hand down her shoulders, stroking her arms, then slowly drew his hands around her lower back down to her bottom squeezing both her bum cheeks.

Kia was now turned on and breathing heavily. As she gasped, she wrapped her arms around the back of Derrick's neck and lifted her chin up indicating Derrick to kiss her neck. Derrick obliged, softly biting and sucking the right side of Kia's neck.

She squeezed her eyes closed as if she couldn't bear the intensity. She whispered into Derrick's left ear, "Fuck me." Wearing only a silk shirt nightie that ended beneath her thighs, it was easy for Derrick, now fully erect, to access her.

Caressing Kia's smooth arse cheeks, he raised the nightie, picked her up by her bottom and sat her on the table. With her legs now around his waist, Derrick entered her soaking wet vagina with his erection and began to slowly fuck her while biting her neck at the same time. Kia loved this.

They made love in the kitchen for hours before finally conking out naked on the couch.

The next day the weather was rainy with strong gusts of wind. It was now 10.30 in the morning and Derrick and Kia were on their way to Kia's twin sister's home. Scheduled to be there for 11am, despite bad traffic they were on track to be on time.

Driving as fast as he safely could in his Range Rover, Derrick and Kia listened to classical music as they travelled to their destination.

Derrick's love for classical music had rubbed off on Kia. She used to find the music boring; she was more of a hip hop and 90's R&B music fan but had started to appreciate the soothing and relaxing effects of classical music, and Kia needed to be relaxed.

It had been seven years since she had last seen her twin. Kia knew that it was very unusual for twins to be separated for so long, but she and Shereece were not your usual twins. Much had happened in both their lives. Their mother had died giving birth to them and as a result, their father, Mark Corret, had raised them as a single parent.

Mark was a six-foot tall, white, bald-headed Scottish man with a thick brown moustache. He was also a successful business owner of a coffin and undertaking business. He ran his business from home, storing the coffins in the house's huge basement. Rumours went around in the neighbourhood about the Corret family.

People gossiped about the relationship Mark had with his daughters. He was very clingy and protective of his daughter, Shereece. He would never let her leave the house without him and up to her first year in college he would pick her up and drop her off to school.

They did everything together but his relationship with Kia was very different.

With Kia he was less strict and allowed her to have her independence. He never really built up a relationship with Kia. He gave her a monthly allowance and every now and again asked her about school but that was it. He never asked her anything about her personal life and seemed to mostly avoid her.

On one particular occasion, Kia had the guts to openly question her father about the different way he treated her from her sister. They were 14 years old and the end of year school party was occurring. "Dad, I want to go to the school party with Kia," Shereece said.

"You aren't going nowhere, now get back upstairs!" Mark screamed in his Scottish accent.

"Why can't she come?" Kia bravely asked, stepping in on her sister's behalf. "The whole school is going to be there. It will look silly if I turn up and she doesn't," said Kia.

It wasn't usual for Kia to defend her sister. Kia was a confident, good looking, heavy make-up wearing, popular 14-year old while Shereece was the total opposite of that. She was shy, reserved, unconfident, and into her school books.

At 15 stone she was very big and considered unattractive by her peers. It was amazing to know they were twins as they were so different. They were fraternal rather than identical twins and their facial features were alike only if one closely scrutinized their faces.

Although Shereece was fond of her twin and wanted to be closer to her, Kia didn't feel the same way and normally neglected Shereece. But on this occasion she felt differently. She felt it wasn't fair for her sister to not be allowed to go to the school disco when she was. Shereece obediently fled upstairs after her father snapped at her.

"Why do you always want her to stay so close to you?" Kia asked her father in a low tone as she squinted her eyes at him in suspicion, she was genuinely curious.

Turning to look Kia dead in her eyes Mark raised himself up off the couch and walked towards Kia who was at the door of the living room. Standing two feet away from Kia, Mark sharply asked, "What did you say to me?"

Kia was intimidated by her father's presence in front of her. She felt a heavy slap to the face would be heading her way if she dared utter another word and dashed through the front door and out the house.

Chapter 3

Moving in

"Pull into that driveway Derrick," Kia said. Kia stood in front of the porch after Derrick had parked and stared at the front door with a nameplate which read *'Corret residence'*.

"Are you ok Kia?" Derrick asked whilst putting his arm around his wife's shoulders. "Yes Derrick I'm fine, it's just been a long time that's all."

"Come on," said Derrick encouragingly as he nodded his head towards the house. Kia took a deep breath then pressed the doorbell twice. Before a full minute passed they heard footsteps hastily coming to the door. They heard several door locks being unlocked before the door pulled open.

Standing in front of Derrick and Kia was a five foot eight, masculine, mixed raced woman with broad shoulders and long hair extensions that were tied to the back of her head. She was wearing a black tracksuit with black slippers to match. Her name was Shereece, Kia's twin sister.

Shereece stepped towards Kia and threw her arms around her in a hug before kissing her right cheek. Kia returned the hug slowly while rubbing Shereece's back.

"Such a long time!" Shereece said looking at her sister.

"Yes, it has been," replied Kia. Then she looked Shereece's body up and down.

"You look so toned Shereece, oh my gosh, what have you been doing?" Shereece laughed. "Derrick, this is my twin sister, Shereece."

'Twin sister-in what world?' Derrick thought to himself.

Derrick was stunned at how different in resemblance the pair were. They looked nothing alike. Kia was slim, petite and very pretty, Shereece on the other hand looked very butch. She had a square jaw and a manly, muscular figure.

"You must be Derrick," Shereece said as she hugged him. "Come in, it's cold outside," said Shereece as she ushered them in through the corridor, then to the front room that was ahead of them. "Sit down, I've prepared food," said Shereece politely.

The living room floor had been renovated since Kia last saw it. Pictures of their parents were on the wall, Mark Corret and his deceased wife Ebal Corret.

Ebal was a short, beautiful, black Ghanaian woman who wore her hair in thick cornrows. Shereece had left the house walls and pictures the same as when their father resided in the house.

The property belonged to their father, but since he had walked out on the girls fourteen years ago and hadn't been seen since, the twins had lived in the house alone until Kia independently moved out and got her own place two months after he left, leaving Shereece to live in the house alone.

After Kia left the house, she never returned. She never wanted to live with her twin and although she had her reasons why she didn't want to be around her sister; now as a grown woman she felt a sense of guilt for having been so distant from Shereece. Kia now wanted to be there for her.

"I'm so sorry about your miscarriage Shereece," said Kia walking towards Shereece to hug her.

"It's fine. I'm in quite a lot of shock about the news that's all Kia. I really felt I wanted to be close to you at this time," Shereece replied with her voice full of emotion.

"You'll be ok Shereece," said Derrick. "It's really common for a woman to not be able to carry a child to full term, but there's so many alternatives, plenty of surrogate mothers and-"

"Derrick!" Kia cut Derrick off with a sharp look in her eyes, as if to signal that Derrick was being insensitive.

"I don't think Shereece needs to hear that right now," said Kia.

Derrick took a glance at Shereece for a few seconds, then said, "I'm sorry. I'll go and bring in the luggage from the car."

"We're going to spend as much time with you as possible, Shereece, until I'm content you're ok."

"You don't have to do that Kia. I mean I really don't want to inconvenience you, as I know you've got work with your busy salons and things."

"Don't be silly," Kia replied whilst looking in Shereece's eyes. "You're my sister, what are sisters for? Besides, this will give us the opportunity to spend time together. We haven't spent time together in years," Kia said whilst holding her sister's hand. They both shared a smile.

The twins' father went missing when Kia and Shereece were 16 years old. He left one day and never came back, leaving behind a note reading, *'I'm sorry I have to go, I know I've been a terrible Dad and no longer believe in myself to be around. I have found a woman and will be starting a new life with her. Shereece, you are by far my best creation. You're my beautiful princess. I love you but I am not competent of raising such an angel. I have not got over the death of your mother and I can't bear to look at or be around Kia.*
It was her fault that your mother died. She caused the birth complications while your mother was pushing her out of her womb.
That little devil bitch took away the love of my life. I can't get over it and I can't forgive her. I don't care if she reads this Shereece. She's a curse. We would have had a whole family if not for her. Do not attempt to look for me. One day I will return to your life Shereece. Love, Dad.'

The note brought shock and disbelief to Kia. At first she didn't believe it, but the handwriting was definitely her father's. Shereece didn't doubt the letter.

After handing the wrinkled note to Kia, she sat down on the kitchen chair and stated, "I knew something like this was coming. He had said this to me before Kia. He told me he'd leave us one day and abandon this house because it depresses him."

But Kia was still baffled, shocked and confused. The letter was cold and blunt towards Kia. It broke her emotionally and it now made sense to her why her dad had avoided her throughout her life.

After several weeks had gone by and Mark still hadn't returned home, Kia moved out of the house into her friend's flat. Not being able to stay in the family house anymore, she felt she had no family and from then on mentally told herself she was alone in this world and cut off all contact with Shereece; leaving Shereece to live in their father's property alone.

A few hours had now passed since Kia and Derrick had arrived at the house and it was now 5pm. Derrick had put all the luggage in the bedroom where he and Kia would be staying.

It was a nice large bedroom. There were three bedrooms in the property and Shereece insisted her sister and Derrick stay in the largest one. Kia had told her sister she wanted to cook for her and wouldn't have it any other way.

While Derrick and Shereece were sitting at the kitchen table, Kia began rummaging through the fridge and cupboards bringing out chopped tomatoes and mince beef. "No spaghetti?" Kia said to Shereece.

"No sorry, there isn't."

"Don't worry, I'll quickly nip to the store and pick some up," said Derrick.

"Yeah we can all go together," said Kia.

"No, you both stay here I'll go," asserted Derrick. Kia looked at Derrick with a stony expression on her face that spoke a thousand words. The look was as if to express disappointment and fear simultaneously.

"Ok no problem, Derrick, I'll stay with my sis," Shereece said.

"Ok, would you like anything Shereece?" Derrick asked.

"I'm fine, thanks Derrick," Shereece replied.

"Would you mind getting me a twenty pack of B&H fags also?" asked Kia.

"I thought you'd given up?" said Derrick. Kia looked at Derrick with a let's not get into this expression on her face. Derrick got the message, smiled and nipped off to the store whilst Kia and Shereece went into the living room.

"I really appreciate this," said Shereece to Kia. "I always knew there was something wrong with me inside. I purposely never used contraception because I wanted to fall pregnant." Kia stayed silent listening to Shereece as the mince beef was defrosting in the kitchen.

She started stroking Shereece's arm in comfort as they sat on the living room sofa. Shereece went on to ask, "Why have things never gone right for me Kia? I've never been successful with friends or men or even jobs, and now this.

I can't even have a fucking baby!" Shereece said angrily. "And you Kia, you've always been the opposite from me, so sociable, successful with men, popular with everybody, beautiful looking. You're so great Kia. Things have always gone so well for you and bad for me. I guess I'm just the shit rubbish twin," Shereece said before bursting into tears.

"Oh no," Kia said and hugged her twin in condolence. "You're gorgeous just like me," Kia chuckled. "Don't kick yourself, Shereece. You're being ridiculous."

"I'm so not. I envy you Kia and I feel so guilty for that."

"You shouldn't feel guilty. If you just-" SNAP! Before Kia could finish her sentence, Shereece grabbed both collar sides of Kia's t-shirt so tight that Kia's skin was cut from the stretch of her shirt.

"I spent years of my life envying you Kia, years! I just want to say I'm sorry. I got you all wrong," Shereece said before loosening her grip on Kia and hugging her tightly.

"I love you Kia," Shereece whispered in Kia's left ear. Kia, still half frozen from Shereece's unexpected grip hold remained stiff and silent, but then Shereece broke the short silence by saying, "and you love me too, don't you Kia?"

Kia slowly hugged her sister, and her face expression formed a slight smile. She then replied,

"Yes Shereece, I do, that's why I am here. We're twin sisters, Shereece, and we've got to have each other's backs, right?"

"Yes we do, forever."

Twenty minutes went by before Derrick rang the doorbell.

"That must be Derrick," said Kia. Shereece got up from her sofa to answer the door. She opened the front door to see a soaking wet Derrick from the pouring rain.

"Flipping hell, it's terrible out there," said Derrick as he strolled through the front door.

"That Bolognese you're cooking Kia better be great to make that trip worth it," Derrick whined as the twins both laughed, looking at Derrick's soaking face. Shereece took Derrick's coat off his back and went to hang it up.

"Kia has been filling me in on everything about you Derrick," Shereece humorously lied.

"Oh yeah? She's telling you what a great guy I am, is she?" They all laughed.

"You're so full of yourself Derrick," said Kia.

Chapter 4

Gasping for Air

"Kia," Derrick called out to his wife lying next to him. It was now midnight. They had all earlier enjoyed the spaghetti Bolognese Kia had cooked, and had fun playing card games. Shereece then hugged, kissed and thanked them both before going to bed. Kia and Derrick went to the bedroom Shereece had made up for them.

"Maybe we should pick some more clothes up from home tomorrow?" Derrick suggested. They had only packed enough clothes for a few days, but given the warm welcome they had received, Derrick felt that they might end up staying for longer than they initially intended.

"Yes hon," Kia replied to her husband who was now reading a thriller book with the lamp on. Kia had been in deep thought and hadn't spoken since she came to bed. Derrick picked up on this. It played on his mind earlier how Kia looked at him with a horrified expression on her face when he insisted she stay while he went to the store.

"Why did you look at me funny when I suggested that you stay at home with Shereece while I popped to the store?"

"Funny, how?"

"Funny, like I said something wrong Kia. I mean you should have seen your face."

"I don't know what you're on about Derrick."

"Kia I-" were the only words Derrick managed to get out of his mouth before Kia cut him off.

"I'm tired Derrick and would just like to go to sleep now," said Kia rolling over, giving Derrick her back.

Derrick wasn't the type to push on small issues he felt may erupt into an argument. Instead, Derrick stared at her bewildered. 'Why was Kia being so evasive, and what was that look about earlier?' Derrick wondered. It was clear something was wrong.

Derrick continued to read his book until he eventually fell asleep. 3am that same night, Kia began softly elbowing Derrick. "Derrick, Derrick, wake up," Kia said while elbowing Derrick's arm. Derrick awoke fighting to open his eyes.

"What's wrong babe? What time is it?" Derrick asked looking at the clock that was on the cabinet behind Kia. It was too dark to see so Derrick switched on the lamp light. He looked at the time. Kia sat up with her arms crossed staring at her thighs with a focused expression on her face.

"There's something I need to tell you Derrick."

"Sure babe. What's wrong? What's up?"

"There's something you don't know about me and my sister, something I haven't told you." Kia was now looking Derrick in his eyes and her facial expression was serious. Derrick remained silent, waiting for her revelation. "Years ago, when we were young and in our teens, my sister"..... Kia took a deep breath and looked Derrick in his eyes.

"My sister tried to kill me."

"WHAT?" Derrick replied in a heavy whisper. "What are you talking about? How?" said Derrick in a confused state.

"Right, in high school there was this guy named Michael I had a crush on. I think at the time he liked me too, but none of us made it known. The problem was my sister liked him as well.

One day after school, me and two of my best friends at the time, Jemma and Leanne, along with my sister were walking home together. Michael and two of his friends, Craig and Cameron, were also with us.

There was a park near ours and it was a nice day so none of us really wanted to go home just yet, so I suggested we all go to the park and hang out for a bit, and that's where we all ended up. Shereece didn't usually come back home with me. She usually went home with my dad, plus we both had our different set of friends, but that day was different.

The boys had gotten some bottles of alcohol, cigarettes and weed. Hours passed and we were all drinking and smoking. Oh my God, we were having such a great time. Shereece didn't smoke anything but she took some of the brandy. I knew she didn't really want to as I knew what she was like. She was very boring in general, and quiet, but Michael was there and she wanted to impress him. She had told me she liked him previously. I didn't tell her I secretly liked him too, in fact I joked with her, telling her to grab him off the market, but honestly, I knew she wasn't attractive enough to bag Michael. Michael was cute and fairly popular amongst the boys. I knew his standards were higher than what Shereece had to offer.

Anyway, I can't remember who came up with the truth or dare, spin the bottle game, but we started playing it. We were all saying truth, but when the bottle landed on Michael, he requested a dare. 'I dare you Michael to kiss one of the twins, you can only pick one,' said Jemma. 'FUCK!' I thought to myself. Stupid bitch! She knew that me and my sister both fancied the shit out of Michael, that's why she deliberately dared it.

By now I was very nervous. Even the brandy and weed couldn't numb the nerves in me. Michael had a wide smirk on his face like he was happy to get the dare. 'What if he does choose my sister,' I thought to myself. 'What if I'm wrong and she is his type, after all we all have different tastes.'

I would have been gutted if he had chosen to kiss her and not me, but at the same time I would have been happy for her as she didn't get any attention from boys at all. But that didn't happen. Michael walked up to me, lifted my chin up for my lips to reach his and slowly put his tongue in my mouth. We started kissing like we had been in a relationship for years. It was the best kiss I had been given so far'.

Jemma watched with a smile on her face, but Shereece stared in horror. 'Whoop! Whoop!' Jemma and Cameron cheered. 'So, when you both getting married?' Jemma said out loud, laughing. Me and Michael then both unlocked lips. Shereece had a look on her face as if she had just witnessed the world burn. Her face had gone red. She went quiet and remained so for the rest of the evening.

Nobody took much notice of Shereece and how she may have been feeling, instead we carried on laughing and joking. Shereece wasn't socializing. The kiss had made me kind of shy around Michael and I opted to leave. Me and Shereece headed home. On the way home I asked Shereece if she was ok and if she enjoyed the evening. She told me she was fine and asked me how my kiss with Michael was. I told her it wasn't bad and giggled. When we made it home, Shereece said nothing for the rest of night.

That night we both went to bed at the same time. I fell asleep thinking about nothing but Michael and that luscious kiss. I went to sleep with a smile on my face. I was fast asleep pleasantly dreaming about the day I had and then, and then..." All of a sudden, Kia burst into tears.

"What? Kia what happened?" Derrick asked in concern as he put his arm around her shoulders. Kia was still sitting bolt upright and staring ahead. Her eyes were full of tears which started rolling down her cheeks.

"What happened, Kia?" Derrick asked again.

"All of a sudden," Kia continued, "I was choking, gasping for air. My neck was tightened. I couldn't breathe. My vision was blurry. I remember seeing the room spinning. I reached for my neck struggling to ease the tightening.

I remember thinking, OH MY GOD, it's a belt tightening around my neck! I'm going to die, was the thought running through my head. I couldn't breathe at all.

I managed to struggle upright and see the room's reflection in the mirror in front of me. The reflection showed my sister behind me. She was strangling me with a belt. I couldn't believe it. I couldn't see much because of the darkness, but the moon shining through the window allowed me to make out the anger on her face. I will never forget her face. Her teeth were gritted. Her eyes tightly squinting. She was so angry and strong. I couldn't loosen her grip. I finally managed to let out a faint scream loud enough for my father to come bursting into the room."

"Oh my God Kia, I don't know what to say," said Derrick.

"My dad grabbed her off of me but struggled to restrain her. She was wild and hysterical. My sister had never been like that before. I was shocked and scared."

"Wow," Derrick said shaking his head in disbelief.

"Now you understand why all these years I've tried to avoid spending time alone with her. When she would call me to come over after I moved out, I would make up some lame excuses for why I couldn't come round. I've never fully trusted her after that incident. I hated her for some time after that. But after time passed, I did start to feel a bit guilty for shutting her out of my life. Even though what she did was deep, we were kids, she was young, and people change, right Derrick?"

"Oh yeah, I guess so," replied Derrick sounding doubtful despite agreeing with his wife.

"She's my twin sister Derrick, my only sibling and I love her, that's why I made this choice to visit and spend time with her in her time of need. It's time for me to put the past behind me. I mean, I'm sure everybody is capable of a moment of madness"..... Derrick stared Kia in the eyes, indicating that a moment of madness was an understatement.

"Ok well, maybe a big moment of madness," Kia said laughing. Derrick laughed with her, then they hugged. Derrick hugged Kia tightly as she laid her head on his chest. "You're not saying much."

"I'm just shocked at that revelation Kia."

"Are you thinking of running out the house now that you know about that incident?"

"Yeah, either that or I'm taking all the belts out of this house right now." Derrick and Kia both laughed at that joke. "So, what exactly happened after that incident? I mean how did you live together after that?" Derrick asked.

"We never spoke for like six months after that night. Things were very awkward between us, but one day Shereece pulled me aside and sat me down to apologise.
She said she didn't know what came over her that night and she was very remorseful. She went on to compliment me by telling me how beautiful I was. She told me she envied me and that she wished she was me at times. Shereece had always been insecure and lacked confidence. I felt sorry for her as she spoke. She was being really open with me. She told me I should go with Michael and she would be fine with it. I never did get with Michael though. I tried to boost Shereece's confidence, telling her she was as beautiful as me, and that she has to acknowledge that she is. Be more confident with yourself, I would tell her, let your hair down and don't be so closed off. Reading books and studying was what my sister was good at. She was very preoccupied with school. I would tell her to step out of the boffin world a little. She agreed and hugged me. She told me she loved me and would never hurt me again."

"That's crazy. I mean what she did, but family is everything and it was a long time ago. You two are twins and twins should be close. What you're doing now Kia, is great. You should build a bond together. I'm going to give you all the time you need to get close to your sister."

"I love you Derrick. You're so supportive, and you say the right things at the right times,... well maybe not always." They both laughed. Kia was looking into Derrick's eyes while expressing her feelings towards him.

"I'm so lucky to have you." Kia then brought her lips to Derrick's mouth.

They both began kissing passionately. Derrick then proceeded to lift off Kia's nightie, undressing her until she was fully naked and they made love.

The next morning Shereece came into the room Derrick and Kia were sharing. "Hey, wakey wakey!" Shereece said loudly while opening the curtains to let the sun beam in.

"What time is it?" Kia asked covering her eyes.

"9am," replied Shereece. "So, no plans for you to be somewhere today then Derrick? It is Saturday. I don't want you to waste your evening with us two ladies. Invite your friends up to the county and go out for a drink. There are loads of good hotspots round here, ain't that right Kia?" said Shereece. Shereece looked at Kia, Kia looked at Shereece, then looked at Derrick, Derrick looked at Kia. There was a short silence. Shereece was clearly hinting for Derrick to leave the house and give her and Kia the evening to themselves. Kia broke the silence.

"Yes Derrick, there are some nice spots around here. You should go out somewhere."

'Wow,' Derrick thought to himself. Kia was happy for him to leave her and her sister alone together. She must now feel comfortable with Shereece.

'This is good,' thought Derrick. He honestly didn't want to spend the whole weekend in the house with them both anyway. He felt that they needed time together alone to talk and to bond without him being in the way, so he went along with it.

"Great, I'd love to check out this area. My mate, Zack, lives in Colindale about twenty minutes from here. I'm sure he'll be up for going for a drink this evening."

"Yeah, do that. Me and Kia will be fine." Derrick took one more glance at Kia in order to get the ok.

"Yes Derrick we will be cool," said Kia.

Chapter 5

Broken Vase

It was now 6pm. Derrick arranged to meet Zack and had left the house at 5pm. Kia and Shereece were now alone together. After watching a few soaps, the sisters began talking about old and present times. "So how are things between you and Derrick?" asked Shereece.

"Great. Derrick is such a great guy. I couldn't ask for more. He's so supportive of all the decisions I make, especially with the salons. I don't think I could have managed to get the salons without him."

"Really?"

"Well, he bought the first one for me, didn't he? Where was I getting money from to open up a salon?" laughed Kia.

"That's how sweet he is Shereece. After me going on about my dream of having my own salon and trying to save up to open one, he stepped in and put the money up for me, and that's how Nazshihair got started."

"Nazshihair? Where did that name come from?"

"I named it after a friend who passed away in university."

"Oh, I'm sorry to hear that Kia," said Shereece as she placed her hand on her heart with empathy.

"It's ok. It was a long time ago," Kia said with a hint of sadness in her voice.

"Well, I'm really happy for you with your salons and all."

"Aww thanks, Shereece."

"I'm going to make some tea. Do you want one?" Shereece said while getting up from the sofa.

"Yeah babes, I'll have one." Shereece left the living room and headed to the kitchen. "How many sugars do you have!"?!" said Shereece loudly from the kitchen.

"Two please......I'm going to find the perfect man for you Shereece! You need a boyfriend who's serious about settling down, and I'm going to hook you up!"

As Kia went on, Shereece silently mimicked Kia's voice, as if to express disgust of her sister going on about hooking her up with a man and how good her own life and boyfriend were. Shereece made Kia's tea then walked into the living room with it.

"Here you go Kia," said Shereece as she handed Kia the hot cup.

"Thank you darling." Shereece then went back into the kitchen apparently to get her own tea.

Kia was your typical pretty faced match maker type of woman who enjoyed romantically hooking people up. She was going through her phone, running through a list of male friends she knew from her husband's colleagues to personal friends who she thought may suit her sister.

"Hmm, Adrian's nice looking, but he's a player so no," Kia laughed to herself. She was truly in her own little world thinking out loud, going through men in her phone and in her head to match with her sister.

Meanwhile Shereece was in the kitchen, but instead of making her cup of tea, she picked up a tall heavy ceramic vase from her kitchen counter, taking it with her out of the kitchen and headed for the living room.

Kia was still talking out loud, sitting on the sofa with her back to the kitchen. Shereece slowly walked up behind her with a serious expression on her face holding the vase tightly in her hands.

"So how about Jonathan Shereece? He's a gentleman, no kids, 33, single, only thing is he still lives with his mum,"

Kia chuckled. “But he has potential, decent looking too. By the way, what is your type Shereece? I mean looks wise.... Shereece?... Shereece!”.....Hearing no reply, Kia turned her head and was shocked to see Shereece's huge figure right behind her raising what appeared to be something heavy in her hands. Kia managed a gasp before, SMASH! Shereece slammed the vase right down on Kia's head knocking her clean out.

Shereece then proceeded to drag Kia's body across the living room floor and down to the basement where the twins’ father used to store all the coffins for his business.

The basement had a trap door that was on the left-hand side of the living room floor but this couldn’t be seen as it was camouflaged by the oak living room flooring and also by the single sofa placed above it.

Shereece handcuffed Kia’s wrists and shackled her ankles before putting her body in one of the coffins. She then went back to the living room to clean up the broken vase and the blood that had trickled down from Kia’s head onto the floor. After cleaning up the mess, she returned to the basement to nurse Kia’s head.

Several hours had passed before Derrick returned to the house. Derrick pressed the doorbell twice. "Derrick, Derrick!” Kia screamed out. Now fully conscious, she was desperate to get Derrick’s attention to both warn him and save herself.

"Shut the fuck up!" said Shereece before closing the lid of the coffin she had bundled Kia into. She then took a remote control from her black desk drawer and used it to switch on a monitor above her head that was connected to the corner ceiling of the basement.

Next to the monitor was a bell that rang when the doorbell was pressed. The monitor showed the top of Derrick’s head and face.

Shereece made her way to the top of the basement stairs, then opened up the trap door and came out. "Coming!" she shouted out, hastily running to her front door. Derrick rang the doorbell again. Shereece made it to the door and opened it fully. "Hi Derrick, come in. You alright?"

"Yeah I'm fine. I was getting worried about you both. I've been trying to call Kia's phone but it's just been ringing out. Where is she?"

"Oh, we must have had the music on too loud. I was playing her Adele's new album. You want a drink?" Derrick noted that Shereece had not given him an answer as to where Kia was. Derrick walked into the living room only half sober. He and Zack had been drinking at the Lion's gate lounge, a popular local bar in the county.

"So where is Kia, Shereece? Is she in bed upstairs?"

"No, she's just popped out to buy me some fags."

"To buy you some fags?" Derrick slowly repeated with a bewildered look on his face.

"Yes," said Shereece smiling whilst looking Derrick in the eyes, "I ran out of cigarettes and she insisted she go and buy me a packet. I wanted to go but she wouldn't allow it. She wanted to walk to her old neighbourhood shops again. She'll be back any minute now. Sit down, you look like you need a rest, Derrick," Shereece said as she ushered Derrick to the sofa.

Derrick didn't resist, he really was in need of a rest, and slumping on the sofa was a lush feeling. Although it didn't quite add up to why Kia would go wandering to the shops alone at such a late hour. Intoxicated by all the vodka shots he had been drinking, Derrick's focus was on getting sober.

"I've had more than I should have to drink Shereece."

"What are you like?" Shereece giggled. "I'll get you some water and you'll be fine." Shereece headed to the kitchen fridge and took out a bottle of fresh cold Volvic water. She prepared a glass of water for Derrick, then looking over her shoulder to make sure the coast was clear, she dropped a tablet of the powerful tranquiliser, Rohypnol, into the glass. After making sure the tablet had fully dissolved into the glass of water, she walked into the living room and handed Derrick the glass.

"Ahh thanks Shereece. Derrick took a big sip of the water before putting the glass down on the dining table.

"Ahh, that was needed. You should have gone to the shop with Kia Shereece. At this time of the night, she shouldn't have gone alone."

"She'll be fine Derrick. She's probably on her way back right now."

"Ok," Derrick replied with a sigh.

"You look really tired Derrick."

"I could do with a nap." Shereece started staring at Derrick, desiring his handsome face. Derrick had his eyes closed and looked like he was in a dream world. Shereece knew that the drug she had spiked Derrick's drink with took at least 30 minutes to kick in, but seeing Derrick going swiftly from worrying about Kia to being quiet with his eyes closed as if he was meditating, Shereece thought maybe the drug had taken effect sooner than expected.

Ten minutes had passed, and Derrick hadn't said a word, in fact he was full blown sleeping now.

"Derrick....Deeerrick," Shereece said out loud, but he gave no response. Derrick was mildly snoring now. Shereece moved over to Derrick and sat on his thighs with her legs around his waist.

She started to stroke his face. Staring into Derrick's face she then began to straddle him moving back and forth, grinding on Derrick, all while he was passed out. Shereece began to slowly kiss Derrick's face moving from the side of his forehead to his lips, eventually swirling her tongue in his mouth. She wanted to taste what her sister Kia had.

She began to undress Derrick, removing his boots and trousers, aggressively ripping off the buttons. She pulled off Derrick's socks and boxers. Naked from the waist down and passed out Derrick was helpless on the couch. Shereece quickly began to undress herself, removing all her clothes. She proceeded to pleasure herself by rubbing her clitoris while simultaneously sucking on Derrick's penis.

Although Derrick was not awake, his manhood became erect. "Mmmm you're a happy boy, aren't you Derrick?" Shereece whispered. Seizing the opportunity, Shereece placed Derrick's erect penis into her now very moist vagina. She sat on top of him and began riding him up and down slowly. After a few minutes passed, she began to speed up, rocking back and forth on Derrick's manhood, then bouncing up and down on it.

"Oooh, ahhh!" Pleasurable moans were being made by Shereece. The faster she bounced, the louder her moans became. "Ahhh, aaahhh, yes! Yes! Derrick!" She was now bouncing on Derrick's erection rough, hard and fast.

"Ahhh yes, yes, I'm cumming! I'm cumming!" Shereece shouted loudly, until finally letting out a great big moan.

"Uuuuhhhhhh," Shereece came all over Derrick's penis. "Uuhhhh," she sighed. She then leaned forward and kissed Derrick on his lips before whispering in his right ear, "That was on the house, Derrick."

Chapter 6

Trapped in Captivity

"Help Hey, where am I!" Derrick yelled. Banging on what appeared to be wood, Derrick was calling out into complete darkness.

Trapped in a box Derrick was unable to stand up, he could only bang and shout for help. "Kia! Shereece! Where the fuck am I!? Get me out of here!" Dazed and confused, Derrick felt like he had been sleeping for hours and had no idea he was lying in a coffin. Suddenly the coffin lid opened and Shereece appeared standing over Derrick.

"Hello Derrick," Shereece said with a crooked smirk on her face. Dressed in a black latex suit with black lipstick on her mouth and black eyeliner around her eyes, Shereece looked like a cross between a goth and a dominatrix. Candles were lit and they provided the only light in the basement.

"What, what's going on?" Derrick stuttered, now realizing he was handcuffed by the wrists and shackled by the ankles.

"Don't worry Derrick, you're safe and so is Kia. But in order to stay safe, you've got to play by my rules and you've got to behave."

"What the fuck is going on?! Where's Kia?! Kia! Kia!" SMACK!

"Shut up!" Shereece said as she slapped Derrick hard across the face.

"Derrick! Derrick it's ok! Please just listen to her!" cried Kia. Recognising Kia's voice but not able to see her, Derrick was now confused and highly worried.

"I am Mistress Lilith, and that is what you will call me by. You answer when I speak to you and you always address me as Mistress Lilith," demanded Shereece.

"Fuck you, you crazy bitch! Get me the fuck out of here!" Derrick yelled at her. SMACK! Shereece whipped Derrick hard across his chest with a heavy leather and metal whip she had in her right hand. "Arrrrrggghhh!"

Derrick screamed out loud. The pain was awful. The whip stung. The pain burned as if flames ran across his chest. A long purple bruise almost immediately came up on Derrick's bare chest.

"Don't you ever disrespect Mistress Lilith!" Shereece shouted fiercely.

"Please don't hurt him!" Kia cried out loud. The pain of that whip made Derrick acknowledge the seriousness of the situation he was in. He now felt obliged to listen to Shereece and be careful about the next thing that came out of his mouth.

"Shereece I...I mean Mistress Lilith. I am your friend. We are your friends. We are here to be your friends. Why are you doing this?"

"Because you owe me. She owes me," said Shereece as she pointed to Kia's coffin. "Our whole lives it's always been about her. Kia the beautiful twin. The popular twin." Shereece walked up to Kia's coffin, and continued,

"The one with the heartthrob boyfriend and all the friends sucking up to her. You forgot you had a sister didn't you Kia?" said Shereece as she peered into Kia's coffin.

"It was always about you our whole lives, and you shut me out. You rejected me as your sister. We're twins. Twins are supposed to be close, and you kept yourself distant from me, and why? Was it that I was too ugly for you Kia? Too shameful to be seen with? Or wasn't I confident enough for your liking? You're such a shallow bitch."

"Shereece!" Kia attempted to reply but was only able to say 'Shereece' before Shereece cut her off and told her, "Shut up! It's Mistress Lilith to you both. I'm not going to remind you again.

I was hurt for years knowing I had a sister that had it all but didn't care to acknowledge me. You have no idea what I went through Kia. You have no idea how your neglect affected my life. All I ever wanted was to be close to you, but now I don't care for that. It's been years since I cared for that. I was angry and hated you Kia, but I was willing to let that hate go if I could just have a child, a baby. A little girl who loved me and depended on my love, who needed me! Nothing else would have mattered. It would be me and my baby and that's all that would have mattered. It would have made me happy. That's all I would have needed. That simple gift nature gives to us for free, but not me. I can't even fucking have that. I can't bear children," Shereece muttered before bursting into tears.

"What is all this got to do with me?!" Derrick yelled out.

"Shut up!" Shereece yelled back, as she marched over to Derrick's coffin.

"Shereece please just leave Derrick out of this! Let him go! Your rift is with me!" Kia cried.

"No .... I need you both. You will both have my child."

"What?" said Derrick in a shocked whisper.

"You will make love and have my child," Shereece repeated.

"Look Shereece, I don't know what you're planning, but please let's end this madness. You need help. You're not well. Derrick is a doctor Shereece, he knows counsellors that can help you. I'm so sorry for you Shereece. Yes I realise I've been a shit sister, and I'm so sorry for that, but"-

"Enough!" Shereece snapped out loud, cutting Kia off. "You will have my child. Both of you will. She'll be just like my own. She'll come from your body Kia, that makes her my flesh and blood too." Shereece kept on referring to this unborn child as if she already knew what the gender was going to be.

"What?" Kia said in a horrified whisper.

"You're crazy Shereece, you really are crazy!" Derrick shouted out. Shereece smirked as she said, "You're breaking the rules Derrick." She then walked over to Kia's coffin and lifted her out. Kia was still handcuffed by the wrists and shackled by the ankles. The cuffs and shackles were extremely secure, obviously very well made, making Kia wonder about the great lengths Shereece had gone into acquiring them and plotting her plan.

Shereece unshackled Kia's ankles warning her not to move. She then began to undress Kia, unbuttoning her jeans. Kia began to struggle and twist her legs making things difficult for Shereece.

"Leave me alone Shereece. What are you doing?! Get off me!" This only made Shereece angrier, and she began dragging and tugging at Kia's jeans more aggressively. "Right, I swear Kia, we can do this the easy way or the hard way!"

"Leave her alone!" shouted Derrick who could hear but not see everything that was happening. Derrick was desperately trying to manoeuvre himself up and out of the coffin, but bound by the tight cuffed shackles on his ankles, his struggle was without avail.

Chapter 7

Prangle's Nursery

Detective Crease and Detective Mary are at Prangles nursery investigating April's disappearance. Detective Crease was a six-foot tall, slim built, black male, 57 years of age with a moustache and beard that had turned grey with age. He had been a Detective for the past 25 years after several years on the police force.

Detective Mary was a short five foot four, slim built, white, blonde haired woman, 32 years of age and had been a detective for the past 2 years. Both of them were assigned to the case of missing April.

They were in the nursery office with the door closed talking to Miss Piper, a short middle-aged white nursery teacher and manager at Prangles nursery. According to statements from other nursery staff, she also happened to be the last person seen with April before her disappearance. Miss Piper, Detective Crease and Detective Mary were all sitting down. "So please tell us, where was April the last time you saw her?" asked Detective Crease.

"We were at a park on a day trip."

"What day, what time, what was the name of the park and where was it?" asked Detective Crease sternly.

"It was Farringdon park in Essex, an activities park a few miles from here where we usually take the kids on outings. The day was May, the 4th, a Tuesday."

"I'll need the full address of that park please," Detective Crease, replied simultaneously jotting the information that Miss Piper had given him down in his notebook.

"Oh yes, yes," said Miss Piper hastily, and then going to a book journal that was on the table separating her from the two detectives, she opened up the book and stopped at one of the pages.

"Here is the park we went to," said Miss Piper as she pointed at the address in the book while handing the book to Detective Crease. "Farringdon park, Essex, postcode CM77 7FJ," Detective Crease said to himself while jotting down more information.

"So tell me Miss Piper, how did you lose sight of April? We understand you were her main carer on that day. Shouldn't you have had your eyes on her at all times?" asked Detective Mary in a condescending manner.

"I was watching her!" Miss Piper said defensively, feeling the heat from the detective. "If you were watching her then you would know how she disappeared," said Detective Crease.

"Oh My God. There were so many kids we had to look after that day. I really don't know how April disappeared," said Ms. Piper.

"After talking to your colleagues, we know you were the last person with April that they can recall, is that correct?" asked Detective Mary.

"I may have been the last member of staff with her but maybe not. Why do I feel like I'm being blamed here? The last I can recall, me and April were playing by the swings in the park. I can remember seeing to Stacey, another one of our infants. She wanted me to push her on the swings, so I did, then when I looked around to see April, she was.....she was gone," said Miss Piper, before bursting into tears.

Detective Crease and Detective Mary looked at each other then looked back at Miss Piper. Detective Crease took a tissue out of his left blazer pocket and handed it to Miss Piper.

"Sorry that you're upset Miss Piper. I'm sure you and this whole nursery are going through a very difficult time right now, but we have to be very thorough with this investigation," said Detective Crease. Miss Piper nodded her head in agreement while wiping her eyes with the tissue Detective Crease had handed her. "So do your infants here all have a main carer of some sort?" asked Detective Crease.

"Yes, they do. I was assigned to April on that day, but April's main carer is usually Shereece, Shereece Corret," said Miss Piper.

"Where is Shereece Corret now?" asked Detective Mary.

"She left the nursery soon after April's disappearance. It was all too much for her. They were very, very close."

"Where was she on the day April went missing?" asked Detective Crease.

"She called in sick that week," replied Miss Piper.

"Oh really?" asked Detective Crease.

"Yes. She said she had been having stomach pains and would not be able to make it to work for that week." Detective Crease began jotting down the information in his notebook while Detective Mary looked at Miss Piper with a concerned expression on her face.

"Do you still have Shereece's contact details?" asked Detective Crease.

"Yes, it will still be on our personnel file. I'll collect it for you," said Miss Piper as she got up to leave the room.

"Thank you," replied Detective Crease. When Miss Piper left the room, Detective Crease turned to face Detective Mary. "Shereece will be an interesting person to speak to," he said.

"Yeah, she will be," replied Detective Mary. Then there was a moment of silence. A few minutes went past before Miss Piper reappeared in the office with a form containing Shereece Corret's contact number and address. She gave the form to Detective Crease and pointed to Shereece's information.

"Thank you," said Detective Crease. He then began copying Shereece's details in his notebook. "You might want to make a copy too, Mary," said Detective Crease. After he finished copying down Shereece's details, he handed the form to Detective Mary and she too copied down the details.

"Will there be anything else?" a worried Miss Piper asked whilst still standing up.

"What was Shereece Corret's character like?" Detective Crease asked Miss Piper.

"She was a very motivated nursery worker, always at work on time and interacted well with the kids, especially with April, but she could be too dominant at times," said Miss Piper.

"Dominant? How so?" asked Detective Mary.

"Well, when she wanted things done her way she made herself very clear about it and would sometimes snap if you didn't listen to her."

"Oh really? Can you give us an example?" asked Detective Crease. Miss Piper went to her chair and sat back down.

"There was one time, quite a while back, I was changing April's nappy and Shereece came into the room. She told me she wanted to take over because she felt I wasn't changing her properly.
I told her it was fine and that I had it under control, but she insisted I was doing it all wrong, and before I knew it, she shoved me out of the way and took over. She said, 'This is my child and I know what I'm talking about ok!' Then she just continued changing April."

"She called April her child?" asked Detective Crease in surprise.

"Yes she did," replied Miss Piper.

"Did you not think to sack her for this type of behaviour?" asked Detective Crease.

"I'm just the manager, I'm not the owner, so I cannot sack anybody. You know I've really got to get on with work now. Will there be anything else?" asked Miss Piper, clearly wanting the interview to be over.

The two detectives looked at each other, then Detective Crease looked at Miss Piper and said, "No. That will be it for now. Thank you for your time, Miss Piper," while getting up off his chair. Detective Crease reached out his hand to shake Miss Piper's hand. Miss Piper shook his hand and then shook Detective Mary's hand as well.

They all then exited the office. On leaving the nursery the detectives made their way to the unmarked police car Detective Crease was driving and got into the vehicle.

"Let's go directly to Shereece without calling her. I don't want to risk her avoiding us if she knows we're coming. After all, in my mind, I'm treating her as a suspect right now," said Detective Crease.

"I agree, but we don't have a warrant to enter and search her property," said Detective Mary. "We'll ask if we can enter when we're there, if she says no, she says no. But then, at least I'll feel she's hiding something, and then we can obtain a search warrant."

"Ok." Detective Crease put Shereece's postcode in his satnav and began to drive. After a thirty-minute drive, they arrived at Shereece's premises. Detective Crease rang the doorbell twice. There was no answer. Detective Crease pressed the doorbell again.

"Coming!" shouted Shereece, walking towards her front door. Shereece opened up the door until it caught on the latch and peered through the gap.

"Hi there. I'm Detective Crease and this is Detective Mary," said Detective Crease as he pointed to Detective Mary whilst also showing his badge. Detective Mary also showed hers.

"We're looking for Shereece Corret," said Detective Mary.

"That would be me. How can I help?" replied Shereece.

"We're investigating the disappearance of April Ford. We understand you were her key worker at Prangles nursery," said Detective Crease.

"Yes that's correct," replied Shereece.

"May we come in?" asked Detective Crease.

"Yes, of course," said Shereece confidently. She removed the latch from the door. Detective Crease and Detective Mary both walked into Shereece's house. Both detectives were taken aback by Shereece's muscular physique.

"May we sit down?" asked Detective Mary as they entered the living room.

"Yes sure. Would you both like a cup of coffee or tea?" Shereece asked in a pleasant manner.

"No, no, don't worry yourself, we're fine," said Detective Crease. Shereece sat down on a sofa that was opposite from the detectives. Detective Crease began to scan the living room with his eyes. "This is a nice place you have here Shereece," said Detective Crease.

"Thank you."

"Because you were April's key worker, it's important we talk to you about her disappearance," said Detective Mary.

"Yes that's fine, I understand that. It's terrible that she's gone missing, it's absolutely broken me. So much so that I couldn't bear to do my job anymore," said Shereece.

"Can I ask why you called in sick the week April went missing?" asked Detective Crease.

"I was experiencing terrible stomach pains," replied Shereece.

"Did you go to the hospital or doctors?" asked Detective Mary.

"I, I didn't, no," stuttered Shereece.

"Why not? If you felt sick why didn't you go to the doctors?" asked Detective Crease.

"I didn't think it was that serious," replied Shereece.

"It was serious enough for you to not go in to work," said Detective Mary.

"Look, if you think I was involved in April's disappearance you're barking up the wrong tree, ok. I'd never do anything like kidnap or harm a child. I loved that little girl."

"Well that's what we're afraid of. Maybe you loved her so much you wanted to take her as your own. From what we hear you can be quite possessive Miss Corret," said Detective Crease.

"I didn't kidnap April," said Shereece with a stern expression on her face.

"Do you live here alone?" asked Detective Mary.

"Yes, just me," replied Shereece.

"You wouldn't mind if we have a look around your property, would you?" asked Detective Crease.

"Go ahead I have nothing to hide," replied Shereece.

"How many bedrooms does this house have?" asked Detective Mary.

"Three bedrooms," replied Shereece.

"I noticed you have a CCTV camera on the top of your front door. Any particular reason for that?" asked Detective Crease.

"I've been burgled before and I like to feel secure in my home," replied Shereece.

"Oh, I'm sorry to hear about your break in," said Detective Crease.

"It's fine," replied Shereece. Both detectives walked through to the kitchen.

"What do you do with yourself now, Shereece? Are you working somewhere else?" asked Detective Mary.

"No, I'm not working at the moment. I'm taking time off work for now," said Shereece. "How are you supporting yourself?" asked Detective Crease.

"I have savings!" said Shereece loudly.

"No need to raise your voice," said Detective Crease.

"I'm sorry, I'm just not used to being under pressure with personal questions being asked."

"Well you must understand that a little girl has gone missing, and we have to investigate her disappearance thoroughly," said Detective Crease. There was a short silence. Detective Crease and Detective Mary glanced at each other, then back at Shereece. "We know you were questioned by police already about April's disappearance," said Detective Crease.

"Yes, and I told them everything I know, which is nothing. She went missing on the week I was unwell and that's all I know," said Shereece.

"May we go upstairs?" asked Detective Crease.

"If you must," replied Shereece. Both detectives were led upstairs by Shereece and shown the bedrooms.

When they entered the room Derrick and Kia were staying in, Detective Mary noticed a size 10 timberland boot on the floor that belonged to Derrick. Shereece had forgotten to clear it up and put it in the basement where she had put the rest of Kia's and Derrick's luggage.

"Who does that shoe belong to?" asked Detective Mary, pointing at the timberland boot. Shereece's heart skipped a beat as she secretly panicked.

"Oh, I had a friend staying," said Shereece.

"Where is the other shoe?" asked Detective Crease.

"It must be around somewhere," said Shereece pacing around the room and acting as if she was looking for Derrick's other shoe. Both detectives stared at each other, then back at Shereece. "I really can't believe I'm being treated as a suspect," said Shereece putting her hand on her heart.

"We're just doing our job, Shereece. Finding April is our main concern," said Detective Mary. Detective Crease's phone went off and he answered it.

"You and Detective Mary are needed at the station," said the voice at the other end of the line.

"I'm on duty," replied Detective Crease.

"It's an emergency so if you can, report to the station as soon as possible," said the police lieutenant through the phone.

"Alright," replied Detective Crease before hanging up. "We've got to go," said Detective Crease to Detective Mary. "Well, Shereece, we will be leaving you for now, but if we have any further questions we'll be in touch," said Detective Crease.

"I'll see you both out," said Shereece and walked the two detectives down to her front door. Shereece opened, then closed the door behind them, leant her back to the front door and let out a sigh of relief.

Detective Mary and Detective Crease got in their vehicle and made their way to the police station. "So, what do you think?" asked Detective Mary while Detective Crease was driving.

"To be honest, I think she seemed quite genuine. I mean there is no evidence that suggests she's a suspect other than hearing she can be controlling, but that alone doesn't mean she's a kidnapper."

"We need to start looking for more leads. What did the lieutenant want?"

"He didn't say, he just said we should report to the station asap, it's an emergency." Detective Mary and Detective Crease arrived at the police station. They went to Lieutenant Dean Hackman's office and both took seats.

"Right, there's been another disappearance. A Jewish man by the name of Stuart Green has gone missing. I'm assigning you both on the case to investigate his disappearance and hopefully find the poor bastard because his wife is driving us crazy," said lieutenant Hackman.

Chapter 8

Mistress Lilith

It's 2pm on a Thursday afternoon. Detective Mary and Detective Crease are at the home of Mr Stuart Green, standing in the living room taking statements from his wife Amira Green.

"Mrs Green, were there any holidays or trips your husband mentioned taking?" Detective Mary asked.

"No! Nothing at all!" Mrs Green blurted out. "It is not like my husband to be away this long. I know something is wrong. Something has happened to him, I know it. In our ten years of marriage, he has never been away from me and Lilly for more than twenty-four hours."

Lilly was the couple's 6-year old daughter. Detective Crease looked over at the grey fabric armchair that Lilly was quietly sitting in. She was a beautiful girl with curly, long, brown hair and she seemed quiet and well behaved.

The look on her face showed how worried she was about her father. She sat there anxious and worried as if she was just hoping to hear the detectives say something that would bring the disappearance of her father to a happy conclusion.

Detective Crease felt pity for the little girl and the wife. Judging from the inside of the house he could see that this was a traditional, well-kept family home with family pictures decorating the living room walls.

"Lilly, go upstairs and play with your toys," Mrs Green said to her daughter. Lilly left the room and went upstairs.

“So, run this by me again, Mrs Green. You said when you called the police station that Stuart called you from work when he left the house on 5th February, to say that he would be home late as he was going to see a friend of his for a few hours, is that correct?" Detective Crease asked Mrs Green.

"Yes,” she replied.

"Is it usual for your husband to see friends after work?" asked Detective Crease.

"Yes, it is usual. Well, at first it was unusual because in most of our married life he came straight home after work and spent the evenings with me and Lilly. But more recently, at least two times a week for the last, let’s say four months, he would go to see his friend who had recently moved into town, after work," said Mrs Green.

"Right," Detective Crease said while jotting down all the information Mrs Green was giving him in his notebook. "Mrs Green, this friend of your husband, did your husband happen to mention his name or address, or anything that might give us a clue where to find him so we can talk to him?” asked Detective Crease.

"No," Mrs Green replied, turning her face from Detective Crease to look at the floor as if she was ashamed and embarrassed about something.

“Stuart is a very domineering man and believes a wife shouldn't question her husband about what he does in his private time."

"Do you think he could have been having an affair, Mrs Green?" Detective Mary asked. There was a short pause from Mrs Green. It was apparent to Detective Mary and Detective Crease that Mrs Green was about to disclose some information about her husband. Mrs Green sat down and asked the two detectives to join her on the living room sofa.

"One night, a night when Stuart came home extremely late, maybe 11pm or so, I grew suspicious about this friend that had just moved into town, and began questioning him. He dismissed my questions by just saying his friend had a motor problem and needed a helping hand. I didn't believe him.

We quarrelled that night, but I am a humble woman and I don't like fights or to argue, so I let it go. However, I suspected that he might have been with another woman. So that night, I purposely kept myself awake until Stuart was fast asleep, then went through his trouser pocket where I saw he had left his phone. I took the phone out of his pocket, left the bedroom and went to the bathroom where I began to browse through his messages. The messages were totally innocent from what I could see. I was very relieved.

They were just work related and social conversations with male friends. I felt silly and disappointed with myself for what I was cunningly doing. Never before have I ever felt the need to go through Stuart's phone. Up until then I never suspected him of cheating. But then before I could put Stuart's phone back in his pocket and go to bed, something told me to browse through his recent calls, and that's when I was shocked. My heart began to skip beats and I felt sick with heartbreak."

"What did you see, Mrs Green?" Detective Mary asked with a curious expression on her face.

"It was a name that read... Mistress Lilith. My thoughts began racing through my head. Who and why would my husband have a woman in his phone saved under such a name? I sat on the bathtub stunned for a few minutes, then my instincts told me to write the number down. But before I could do this, I heard Stuart heading towards the bathroom door.

I shoved the phone in my dressing gown pocket and flushed the toilet. He asked me if I had seen his phone and I said 'no' as I quickly walked past him and headed for the bedroom. He followed me in and asked me to call his number from my phone. To cut a long story short, I confessed to him that I had taken his phone and seen the name Mistress Lilith. He went berserk, screaming and shouting at me for going through his phone. I confronted him about the name. He said it was just an employee of his and Mistress Lilith was her nickname. That was his explanation, and as a loyal wife I chose to believe it and try to not let it bother me. But it did bother me," said Mrs Green tearfully.

"However, I didn't bring it up again. And that was that. I wish I had taken down that number! Maybe she knows something. I have been managing the store since his absence. Nobody working at the store seems to know or have heard anything about Stuart's disappearance, and there's nobody named Mistress Lilith working at the store. It's so strange for him to just disappear. His store is his life. He would never neglect his business like this or his family. Nobody has heard anything from him."

"Have you been in touch with his family, mother, etc.?" asked Detective Crease.

"Everybody I know in his family I have contacted. As for this Mistress Lilith, none of his colleagues or friends seem to know anybody associated with him by that name," Mrs Green said.

After jotting all his notes down from the information Mrs Green had given, Detective Crease and Detective Mary assured Mrs Green that they would investigate the matter thoroughly and advised her to get in touch with them if she should hear or see anything involving her husband. They left her with their cards before leaving the house.

"Mistress Lilith," Detective Crease said out loud while driving with Detective Mary in the passenger seat.

"Without his phone, how are we going to contact her?" Detective Mary asked.

"That I don't know. What I'm starting to wonder though, is if these missing person cases we've been assigned to are linked. It would make our job much easier if they were."

"Yeah it would, but they're not linked."

"What makes you so sure?"

"Look at the difference in the people. A 4-year old girl and 37-year old man. It doesn't connect with your typical serial killer."

"That's assuming they are dead. But I hear your point. It's just that Bluendale was such a nice, amicable, quiet town, and all of a sudden since last year I've been seeing more and more missing person cases come through our precinct."

"I hear you on that one. Statistically there has been an uprise in missing cases round here. I don't know what's going on. Such an unpleasant world we live in."

"Yep, it can be unpleasant indeed," said Detective Crease as he nodded his head in agreement.

"If they are connected, whoever is responsible would have to be new in town, right?"

"Either that or somebody who's from Bluendale just decided last year to start acting out his fantasies."

"Or she." Detective Crease turned to look at Detective Mary, paused, then faced the road again.

"Anyway," said Detective Crease with a sigh, "we need to speak to this Mistress Lilith. He's obviously been having an affair with this woman on the side and got her saved on his phone under that code name."

“Don't be so sure about that. I mean what if this Mistress Lilith is an actual Mistress? As in a professional dominatrix. He could have a kinky sub fetish or something," said Detective Mary.

"Well, that would contradict what Mrs Green said about him being a domineering guy, wouldn't it?”

“Not necessarily. Some domineering, powerful people enjoy being submissive in their personal lives.”

“Is that so?”

“Yes it’s so, trust me. Let’s google Mistress Lilith,” said Detective Mary as she got on her iPhone and typed ‘Mistress Lilith Bluendale’ into the Google search engine. A website came up at the top of the Google search engine saying Mistress Lilith dominatrix. Detective Mary clicked on the website as Detective Crease pulled over on a side road.

On the homepage of the website it read ‘Professional Dominatrix Bluendale’ with an ‘enter’ or ‘leave’ option. Detective Mary pressed ‘enter’. Detective Crease peered over at Detective Mary's phone to also view the website. Many options came up including ‘About’ ‘Gallery’ and ‘Dungeon.’

"Click on Gallery," Detective Crease said. Detective Mary clicked on the gallery option. "Oh wow, she's a big girl isn't she, Mary?" said Detective Crease as they both looked at Mistress Lilith’s muscular figure. She was posing in various pictures. It reminded them of Shereece's physique. All the pictures of Mistress Lilith had her face blurred out.

"Why is her face blurred out in the pictures?" asked Detective Mary.

“Is it uncommon for a dominatrix to blur their faces out of their promotional pictures?" asked Detective Crease.

"I really wouldn't know." Most of Mistress Lilith's pictures were of her alone, half naked, wearing dominatrix outfits. One particular outfit stuck out. She was wearing a black PVC bra, black PVC skirt and black thigh high boots standing firm with her hands on her hips and her muscles tensed up.

"She must work out every day to have a muscular figure like that," said Detective Mary.

"I agree. Browse a few other dominatrix websites. See if they all hide their faces." Detective Mary searched on Google for dominatrixes in Essex and several dominatrix websites came up. Detective Mary clicked on several of the websites. They found that of the dominatrix websites four out of the ten they viewed the mistresses had their faces blurred out.

"Hmm so it's not uncommon," said Detective Crease. Detective Mary went back onto Mistress Lilith's website and tapped on the location option. The option only revealed 'Bluendale, CM7,' nothing more.

Under the postcode it read 'call to make booking' with a mobile number displayed under the writing. "We're going to have to call to get the full address details, that's how most of these things work. It's too dangerous for them to just leave their full address out there in the open," said Detective Crease.

"Have you worked on a case involving a dominatrix before?" asked Detective Mary.

"Never, but I have worked on several cases involving escorts, and I'm assuming the process works the same." Detective Crease took his phone out and began to dial the contact number on Mistress Lilith's website.

"You calling her right now?" asked Detective Mary.

"Yes."

Chapter 9

Missing April

Six weeks had passed by since the first night Shereece had made Derrick have sex with Kia in her presence. Having quit working at the nursery, Shereece had now become a full-time dominatrix.

She loved being in power and control of both men and women. She had been working part time as a dominatrix three nights a week in the past, simultaneously having her day job as a nursery teacher, but after she committed the kidnap and murder of April, she had decided to resign from the nursery as she no longer had the desire to look after kids that weren't her own.

She told her boss and co-workers that April's disappearance was too distressing for her to continue. Plenty of campaigns were running in regard to April's disappearance. It was featured heavily in the media. April's parents had made appearances on live television daily news pleading for April's safe return.

There had been many different speculations about April's disappearance from the public. Some even assumed that April's own parents may have been involved with her disappearance. There was a massive police and public search for April.

Shereece had been heavily questioned by police as she was so close to April in the nursery. However Shereece was very intelligent, convincing and also very manipulative. She had also appeared on the television news acting distraught after April's disappearance begging the public to thoroughly search for the missing little girl.

"This is every parent's worst nightmare, and has come as a huge shock to us at Prangles nursery. April is such a lovely little girl, she always had a smile on her face and loved to play with all the other kids in the nursery. Please everybody, just be cautious and keep searching for her. She must be found. She's such a lovely little girl."

Shereece ended her statement by bursting into tears leading to the cameras being moved off her for the live report. The case of missing April remained under investigation.

It was 3pm in the afternoon when Shereece's business phone went off while she was doing her daily work out in her living room.

"Hello, Mistress Lilith here, how will you serve me?" Shereece said, heavy breathing as she answered the call.

"Hello Mistress Lilith, this is Detective Crease here. I would just like to have a brief word with you if you would be so kind." Shereece wondered why the same detective who had visited her over April's disappearance was now calling her business phone.

"Is this a prank call? Because if so I'm about to hang up the phone," said Shereece.

"No please don't, I assure you this is no prank call." Shereece's heart began to panic and she started to have flashbacks to when she abducted April, as she held her mobile phone to her ear. 'Did someone notice me that day?' Shereece thought to herself.

She thought she had planned the abduction of April well enough to pull it off without being traced. She had called in sick for work the same week that the nursery had a day trip to an activities park planned. It was on the day of that trip that Shereece went to the location in advance and discreetly parked up and waited for the nursery group to arrive.

She had been parked up for hours, waiting patiently before spotting her opportunity to abduct April. She approached April wearing a blue baseball cap with the cap pulled down over her forehead in case of any witnesses. However, all the adults and infants were occupied when Shereece approached April on the play swings. "Come on April," Shereece said quietly taking April by the arm. As April turned to look at her, Shereece pulled her cap up just enough for April to see her face.

"Miss Corret!" April yelled out, smiling and delighted to see her key worker.

"Shush," Shereece replied, putting her fingers to her lips. And as quick as Shereece crept up to April, she quickly whisked her out of the park and into her four door Ford Mondeo car. To her recollection nobody had seen a thing. Shereece's attention focused back on reality and carefully waited for Detective Crease to continue speaking. "Hello...Lilith are you still there?"

"Yes, I'm here."

"Oh good. I would just like to have a brief word with you about a missing shop owner by the name of Stuart Green. 'Stuart Green' Shereece thought to herself. Shereece knew Stuart Green only too well. He was one of her regular fetish clients, she had killed him several months earlier during a bondage session.

After tying up Stuart and blindfolding him, Shereece plunged a 7-inch knife through Stuart's chest ten times. She did this purely for the thrill of killing a man. It turned her on to take the life of a helpless man under her dominance. "Do you happen to know a man of this name Lilith?"

"No, I do not know that name at all. Why would you ask me?"

"Well since his disappearance, we've managed to get some information from his phone contacts, and your name and number happened to be one of his most recent contacts," replied Detective Crease.

"Listen Mr Detective Crease, you do know what my profession is right? I'm a dominatrix. Therefore, it's pretty obvious why my number is going be in his phone. I have many clients and I don't keep a track of their names or personal details, I do not recall anybody by that name."

"I'll give you his description," Detective Crease replied.

"He's a five-foot four white Jewish male, slim built, blue eyes and clean shaven. He has short brown hair but always wears his yarmulke cap from what we've been told. Does this description ring a bell?"

"No, to be honest it doesn't."

"Very well, Lilith. Sorry for the inconvenience. If by chance you do happen to come across Stuart Green, please contact your local police station."

"May I ask exactly why you're searching for him? Is he dangerous or done something that I should be afraid of?" asked Shereece in a concerned tone.

"No not at all, nothing of the sort. He's just been absent from his family and work for an unusual amount of time, and his family have now reported him missing, citing his absence as completely out of character."

"Oh right. Well, I hope you find him, and I will be in contact if I can help," said Shereece sounding very genuine.

"Thanks again Lilith, and goodbye." Detective Crease then hung up the phone. Shereece sat down on her living room sofa calmly and went into deep thought.

The body of Stuart Green was lying in one of Shereece's coffins. 'I wonder if they're going to come here and carry out a search?' Shereece wondered to herself.

Detective Crease and Detective Mary had come to her house before regarding the investigation on missing April and were not aware of the secret underground basement. Shereece was confident that her basement would conceal all evidence of missing persons.

The basement was now a sex dungeon with enough space and equipment for all sexual and dominatrix activities to be carried out.

Shackled at the ankles, handcuffed by the wrists and living in coffins, Derrick and Kia were living in a nightmare. They had been given a beeper button each by Shereece which they could press to alert her for when they needed to use the toilet.

Beep! Beep! Shereece's beeper went off from Derrick's device disturbing her as she replied to emails from her clients. She got up from the living room sofa and went to see to Derrick. She opened the basement trap door and descended down to the basement, then went to collect a wooden toilet bowl she kept in the corner of the basement. Shereece then unlocked Derrick's coffin.

"Hi Derrick. This better be about something that needs seeing to," said Shereece, she had warned him previously about pressing the button when he just wanted to talk about being released. "I need to use the toilet for a number two, Mistress Lilith," said Derrick obediently.

"That's fine. Let's get you up," said Shereece.

Shereece raised Derrick up by his arms. She lifted Derrick's bound naked body out of the coffin and placed him on the wooden toilet seat. It always crossed Derrick's mind to bite on Shereece's ear as she hurled him out of the coffin.
The opportunity to do this was there, as his face would come in close contact with her ears all the time when she removed him from his coffin. But the thought of not being able to follow through with the attack kept him from acting on this opportunity. Derrick knew how physically strong Shereece was, and she also carried a gun when she was in the basement. 'What if it goes wrong and she kills me for it?' Derrick thought to himself.

"Poo, you stink," said Shereece. Derrick stared at Shereece's face sharply.

"Well maybe if you punched more than two holes in my coffin lid, and washed me more than every other day, I wouldn't smell as bad," muttered Derrick bravely. Shereece was sitting in her own chair opposite Derrick looking him in the face as he replied. But she stayed quiet. They locked stares for a few seconds before Derrick spoke.

"This can't go on Shereece," said Derrick. Shereece's face immediately screwed up in annoyance. "I, I mean, Mistress Lilith," Derrick corrected himself stuttering, "Kia will not be able to have the baby you want under these conditions."

"Why not Derrick?" Shereece asked inquisitively not wanting to miss out on any information that could prevent her baby being born. "I bathe her daily, I feed her appropriately, all like you advised. I keep her coffin lid open so she can have enough air. Why would she not be able to produce my baby?"

"Shereece, a pregnancy under this distressing condition will more than likely result in a miscarriage!" said Derrick angrily. He was furious. Not only from what he was being subjected to, but also from what his wife was being subjected to, and now the possibility of another life, his own child being taken away from him. He was furious.

"No it won't, Derrick. Kia will deliver my baby in great health." Derrick looked at the ground before saying quietly,

"And then what? What will you do with me once you have your baby?"

"That's enough talking Derrick. We're done here. Now finish your shit so I can clean you up and put you back in your coffin!" said Shereece bluntly.

Meanwhile Detective Mary and Detective Crease are seated in their work vehicle outside Bluendale police station.

"Shereece Corret and Mistress Lilith are the same person. I'm sure of it. Shereece is Mistress Lilith. Their physiques are the same, and their postcodes almost exactly match. No way are there two females with a physique like that based in the same small area. I mean what are the odds?" said Detective Mary to Detective Crease.

"Oh, listen to you. All this coming from the person that said these cases aren't linked," said Detective Crease as he looked at Detective Mary.

"I'm seeing things a little different now."

"Don't worry. I'm thinking the same thing. But there's only one way to find out if Shereece is Lilith. We've got to get Lilith's full postcode and see if it matches Shereece's."

"And how are we going to do that?"

"I have an idea. I can call Lilith posing as a client and that way we can get her full address," said Detective Crease.

"But even if we get the full address, and it turns out to be Shereece's address, then what? We've already visited her premises and there was no sign of any foul play there," said Detective Mary.

"What about that shoe in the bedroom? That could have been Stuart Green's shoe."

"Yes it could have been, but seizing a shoe alone isn't going to be enough to prove anything. Besides, if it is what we think she probably would have cleared it up by now."

"We should go with my idea just so we're certain that they're the same person," said Detective Crease.

"Is this legal?" asked Detective Mary. Detective Crease turned to Detective Mary and said "Do you want to find out if they're the same person or not?" Detective Mary turned her face away from Detective Crease's to face the windscreen.

"Ok, do it," said Detective Mary. Detective Crease got out his phone and scrolled down his contact list until he reached Mistress Lilith's number which he had previously saved. He put 141 before the phone number then dialled it. "I'm calling her on private, so there's a chance she might not answer."

The phone rang out ten times before going to voicemail. Detective Crease pressed 'call' on the number again. Again, the phone went to voicemail after the tenth ring.

"We've got to go to a phone box. It's just ringing out," said Detective Crease.

"There's one right there," said Detective Mary pointing at a phone box across the road from them. They exited the vehicle and crossed the road to the phone box. Detective Crease got in the phone booth while Detective Mary waited outside. He put £2 in the phone box, then dialled Mistress Lilith's number. The call was answered after five rings

"Hello, Mistress Lilith here. How will you serve me?" said the voice on the other end of the line. "Hello Mistress Lilith. My name is Steven and I'll like to place a booking please," said Detective Crease.

"Ok, what time were you thinking?"

"Is 4pm ok?"

"No I'm booked till 5pm."

"Ok 5pm is fine."

"Have I seen you before?"

"No, you haven't."

"What are you into?" Detective Crease froze for a second not knowing what to say. "Hello.... are you there? You better not be some punter wasting my fucking time!" said Mistress Lilith angrily.

"No, no. I'm not. I'm into being spanked," said Detective Crease almost laughing. It was the only thing he could think of in the moment. "I like to be spanked naked with a whip and teased."

"Teased how?"

"Well, it's kind of complicated. I'd much rather discuss it with you in person."

"Ok that's fine. Are you driving?"

"Yes," replied Detective Crease while putting another £2 in the phone box slot.

"Ok, my postcode is CM7 3NU," said Mistress Lilith. Detective Crease repeated the postcode and scribbled it in his note pad. "Call me when you arrive at 5pm and then I will give you my door number," said Mistress Lilith.

"Ok I will do."

"Don't be late!" said Mistress Lilith sternly.

"Oh I won't be."

Mistress Lilith then hung up the phone and Detective Crease hung up the phone and exited the phone box.

"Did you get the address?" asked Detective Mary.

"I got the full postcode but not the door number. It's the same postcode as Shereece's," said Detective Crease.

"Oh my God! Are you sure?" asked Detective Mary.

"Yep, I'm sure," said Detective Crease, as he showed her Shereece's address in his notebook, then he flipped the page to Mistress Lilith's postcode. The postcodes were identical.

"I knew it! I knew it!" said Detective Mary out loud, in excitement.

"I know it's Shereece now for sure even without the address. I recognised her voice. She scheduled an appointment for me at 5pm today and I agreed," said Detective Crease.

"Well, we can't show up."

"Yeah, you're right, it doesn't make any sense to turn up at her door again does it?" said Detective Crease while scratching his chin. "I wonder where in her house she holds her services. Those pictures on her website didn't look like they were taken anywhere in her home," said Detective Crease.

"Maybe she has a basement," suggested Detective Mary.

"Maybe. Come on, let's go and talk to Hackman," said Detective Crease. They walked across the road and went into their station. Detective Crease knocked on Police Lieutenant Dean Hackman's office door.

"Come in," said Hackman. Detective Crease and Detective Mary walked into the office. Lieutenant Hackman was typing away on his computer as they entered his office.

"We think we may have a suspect for missing April and Stuart Green," said Detective Crease.

Hackman stopped typing, took his glasses off, leaned back in his chair and put both his hands behind his head.

Lieutenant Hackman was a white, 54- year old veteran in the force. He was chubby with a beer belly, had short trimmed brown hair with a thick moustache.

"Go on. Who're the suspects?" said Hackman.

"Not suspects. Suspect. We believe that the same person is involved in both April's and Stuart Green's disappearance," said Detective Mary.

"Well....who?" asked Hackman.

"Shereece Corret. A teacher at Prangles nursery. The same nursery April went missing from," said Detective Mary.

"A nursery teacher?" said Hackman in surprise. "What brings you both to this conclusion?"

"We visited Mrs Green at her premises and it turns out that Stuart Green was visiting a dominatrix. His wife had gone through his phone and found a number under the name Mistress Lilith. We figured that Mistress Lilith might be a dominatrix so, we went on Google to check it out. We found a website under the title Mistress Lilith in Bluendale. When we logged on to the website, we couldn't help but notice the similarity with Shereece Corret and Mistress Lilith's body shape," said Detective Crease.

"Body shape? I don't understand."

"Shereece Corret and Mistress Lilith have well-built bodybuilder figures. We are sure they're the same person. We couldn't know for certain because Mistress Lilith has her face blurred out on her website. But then we gave her a call and managed to obtain her postcode, and it is the same as Shereece Corret's.

Now this tells us that Shereece Corret was living a double life. Nursery teacher by day, dominatrix by night. We've spoken to some of Shereece's ex-nursery work colleagues, and it turns out Shereece has a bad temper

Shereece was April's key worker, then April goes missing on Shereece's week off. She was Stuart's dominatrix, and he goes missing. Coincidence, or maybe more. We've been to Shereece's house already and seen no sign of foul play, but if we can get a search warrant to maybe lift off some prints..."

"Hahaha!" Lieutenant Hackman cut off Detective Crease with his laughter and placed both his palms on his desk table as he leaned forward. "Are you two kidding me? You want to get a search warrant based on what you've just told me. A nursery teacher has a bad temper so that makes her a child abductor?" asked Hackman sarcastically.

"Wait a minute," said Detective Crease.

"No, I won't wait any minute. You two geniuses don't even have a motive. So what if this Mistress Lilith and Shereece are the same person, it sure doesn't make her a suspect. We aren't applying for any search warrant based on what you've just told me. You must be out of your God damn minds! Leave my office and don't come back to me unless you've got some proper evidence on these cases."

Chapter 10

Trying to Escape

"HELP! HELP!" Derrick shouted at the top of his voice as he lay in his coffin.

Eight months had passed. Kia was now six months pregnant, dwelling in her coffin that was now being left open for her through the day and night.

Shereece had been taking care of Kia by giving her organic food and leaving her coffin lid open so she could get adequate air. Afraid that Kia would miscarry under poor conditions, she was making sure to take extra care of her.

Things were much worse for Derrick. On top of being sexually abused by Shereece, he was being poorly fed. Shereece had no more use for Derrick, her plan for him to impregnate her sister had been successful. Instead of taking care of Derrick, she had been using him as a sex slave for herself and her clients. She used the basement for her dominatrix work. It looked ever so much the part to impress and satisfy her submissive clients. But little did they know that real corpses dwelt within the coffins.

Instead, it just looked like part of her dungeon display. Shereece had been using some of the empty coffins for clients who were into being held captive and buried alive.

There were so many extreme fetishes Shereece's clients would request, and Shereece was not limited to any. The more extreme the fetish was, the more it turned her on.

Derrick eventually became fed up of trying to contact the outside world, knowing his painful cries for help were only heard by the hard, thick, cemented walls and Kia in the coffin yards away from him.

Derrick began to recall a scene of what he had been subjected to by Shereece three weeks earlier. Shereece had brought a client back down to her basement.

The client requested a forced bisexual session, where he would be made to obey Shereece's orders by being spanked and sexually pleasing another man. She had told her client she had a bisexual male sub working with her that would be the participant. Of course this was a lie, the guy she intended to use for the job was Derrick.

'You be a good boy' Shereece said to him as she placed a red ball the size of an apple in Derrick's mouth and bound it round his mouth with tape. He was blindfolded and he was by now too weak to resist Shereece.

Flashbacks of a middle-aged man sucking Derrick's un-erect penis kept coming to Derrick's mind. Although he couldn't see the activities taking place on him because of the blindfold he had on, he could hear and he could feel.

This abuse happened on several occasions. Derrick had been violated by Shereece using him as a homosexual sex slave. Flashbacks of the abusive noises kept running back in Derrick's mind. He tried to block them out but he couldn't. He knew it was a male that was assaulting him as Shereece directed the sessions very verbally.

"SUCK HIS DICK OFF!" she would order her client. "Yes Mistress," her client would reply, then obey. Eventually, Derrick broke out of his frozen stance and began to cry.

He was in hell. This was by far the worst situation Derrick had been in in his life. He began to resent Kia.

'If I wasn't with her this wouldn't be happening to me,' Derrick thought. 'I'm a successful good-looking guy. I could have any woman of my choice. Why did I end up with a woman who led me to being in this awful situation?'

Kia could hear Derrick weeping. Derrick had heard her in the last eight months weep almost every night, but this is the first time she had heard him. He had been keeping strong for her and him, consoling Kia, letting her know it will be ok, being optimistic and brave for the both of them. Derrick had encouraged Kia to stay hopeful, but he could do it no more. He had lost hope.

"JUST FUCKING KILL ME YOU UGLY TWISTED BITCH! YOU HEAR ME YOU FUCKING BITCH! COME ON!" Derrick screamed out.

"Derrick please don't!" Kia cried out hysterically.

"FUCK YOU! If it weren't for you and your fucking twisted sister I wouldn't be here! I wouldn't be here," said Derrick before crying his eyes out.

"I want to get out of here," he cried. He was weak and losing his mind. "This is Ballshit. We're going to die here. She's going to kill me, then when that baby is born, she's going to kill you too, Kia. She has no reason to let us go. Why would she let us go? She knows we'll go to the police as soon as we're released. She can't let us go. We're going to die here. She's going to kill us both."

"I'm so sorry, Derrick. I know you hate me. I can feel it," said Kia as she wept. She began feeling guilty for having such a terrible sister who could do this to the man she loved.

She felt she deserved Derrick's hate. "You deserve better Derrick. Me and my fucked up family! Believe me on this though baby, we will be found. I know Natalie is going crazy right now looking for me."

Natalie is Kia's best friend. A very confident woman but she had no knowledge of where Shereece lived. Kia was banking on Natalie out of all her friends to find her. 'Eight long months have already passed and yet nobody has found us. Will we truly ever be found?' Kia thought to herself, doubting what she had said to Derrick.

"Listen, Kia, I'm sorry for how I spoke to you. I know you don't deserve this either, but listen to me Kia, nobody is going to find us. If we were to be found, it would have happened already. For all we know, police have already come knocking and Shereece has shaken them off. There's only one way we're going to get out of here, and that's by fighting our way out." Derrick pulled himself back together.

"I was angry and confused a minute ago, but my head is clear now, and I know what I must do. I can get these cuffs around her neck, Kia."

"NO!" Kia said firmly. "Don't Derrick. Please don't. She'll kill you. You won't be able to overpower her."

"Listen Kia she's going to kill us, fighting is the only option. I can't take this anymore. If one more sick fucker puts their hands on me again….." Derrick then went silent.

"Kia, you just need to trust me and work with me here. I know roughly where her body is when she's feeding me. I've been thinking about this for a while now.

Once I've got her at a certain distance, I'll wrap both of these handcuffs around her neck and strangle that bitch to death. I want you to keep her entertained.

Talk to her when she's feeding me so she's distracted. She didn't feed me yesterday, so I know she'll feed me today. She only goes a day maximum without feeding me."

"I'm scared Derrick. What if it doesn't work? I'm so scared," said Kia.

"Just trust me, Kia, and be strong. I'll get us both out of here. I'll get her and I'll get her good. I'm going to kill that bitch."

"Shhhhhhh," Kia said as she heard footsteps above her. Shereece was coming down to the basement. The sound of Shereece's footsteps brought fear to the hearts of Derrick and Kia, they never knew what Shereece would do next.

"Time for dinner lovebirds!" Shereece said out loud while walking down the basement stairs. She seemed to be in a really good mood. When she was in a good mood Derrick and Kia felt more at ease, the chances of being attacked by Shereece lessened when she was in one of her talkative good moods. Shereece was unpredictable and had several sides to her.

When she was in her talkative mood she would go through her day with them as if they were her best friends. Speaking to them so casually and friendly, as if she wasn't holding them captive in a basement. She would complain about people she'd seen littering on the streets or about girls wearing skirts she thought were too short. It was unbelievable how she could be such a hypocrite judging and criticising people when she was this evil, psychotic, kidnapping murderer.

Shereece fed Kia then started to feed Derrick.

"Open wide," Shereece said to Derrick before feeding him a spoon of mashed potato.

Derrick was sitting up in his coffin as Shereece had leaned his body up to feed him. Still blind folded, he was happy to be getting fed but also very nervous. He couldn't enjoy the food because too much was on his mind. His heart was racing, he was moments away from his plan to attempt to free himself and Kia by attacking Shereece.

"Open wide Derrick, we're almost done," said Shereece. Derrick knew he had to act quickly, as Shereece announced the plate was almost empty.

As Shereece put the second to last spoon in Derrick's mouth, Derrick struck out as hard as he could with both his arms swinging to the right, BAAAANG! knocking Shereece off her chair and onto the floor.

BOOF! Shereece hit the floor hard. The blow had caught her completely by surprise. Derrick jumped on her body, feeling she was next to him. Although he was blindfolded, the rest of his senses were very sharp. Fearing she would get up, Derrick put all his strength and weight on top of Shereece to force her down. Shereece began struggling and tried to free herself.

"YOU FUCKING BASTARD! YOU'RE FUCKING DEAD!" she yelled. Kia lay terrified in her coffin hearing all the commotion. As they wrestled on the floor, Shereece put her hand in her pocket hoping to get a hold of her fully loaded berretta handgun.

Derrick could sense she was reaching for something in her pockets. He quickly tried to get there first but due to his lack of sight and limited use of his hands due to the handcuffs he struggled to get there. He instead quickly threw both wrists around Shereece's neck and began to strangle her with the handcuffs he was bound by.

Succeeding with the strangulation, Derrick began forcing every bit of his strength on Shereece while tightening the short chain of the handcuffs on her neck. Shereece was now choking, but her hands were still free. She managed to reach for her loaded berretta, whipped the gun out and aimed it up and behind her. Not being able to see Derrick, she shot only at where she assumed her target was.

BANG! The bullet whizzed past Derrick's ear. "Ahhh!" Derrick screamed out in shock from the gun blast. Shereece arched her head up with her strong neck and twisted her head in order to vaguely see Derrick's face. Seeing Derrick now, she arched her strong muscular arms towards Derrick's face.

This time seeing her target, she pulled the trigger with the gun aimed right for Derrick's face. BANG! The bullet blasted into Derrick's right eye blowing it completely out of its socket.

"Arrrrrrhhhhh!" Derrick screamed out as he let go of Shereece and tried to latch on to his right eye socket. Bleeding heavily, with blood gushing out of his eye socket and in agonising pain, Derrick was now powerlessly shivering on the floor. Shereece got up on her feet. Her right hand gripping her handgun. She aimed it to the side of Derrick's head.

"Say your last goodbyes to your husband Kia," Shereece said still breathing heavily from the struggle.

"Nooooooo!" Kia screamed out. She was blindfolded so couldn't see the commotion but heard everything. Fearing that Shereece was about to execute Derrick she screamed out "NO! Don't!" BANG! BANG! Shereece squeezed two shots into the right side of Derrick's head. One bullet lodged inside of his skull, and the other bullet blew off a piece of his cranium, along with some brain matter, exposing the inside of Derrick's head.

Derrick's body lay on the floor naked and lifeless. "Ahhhhhhhhh!" cries from Kia filled the basement. She knew Derrick was now dead. Sobbing in anguish, Kia was hysterical.

"It's just you and me now Kia.... just you and me," said Shereece as she stood over Derrick's dead body with splatters of blood and brain matter over her face and dress.

Chapter 11

Clients

Three weeks had passed by since Shereece had killed Derrick. Shereece stored Derrick's corpse in one of her coffins. The time is 5pm. Shereece is doing her daily work out in the basement when her business phone starts ringing. "Mistress Lilith here. How will you serve me?" she said as she answered her phone.

"Hi, my name is Colin and I'd like to book you for a service this evening," the caller said at the other end of the line.

"What time?" asked Shereece, still pumping her dumbbell.

"Is 7pm ok?"

"7pm is fine."

"Ok fantastic," replied Colin excitedly.

"What services do you require?" asked Shereece.

"Well, I like to be tied up and dominated. You can have your way with me anyway you see fit once I'm tied up."

"Oooh I like the sound of that," replied Shereece in a quirky voice. "Where did you hear about me?"

"I found your website on Google."

"My rates are £200 per hour, £150 for every hour after the first."

"Yes, that's totally fine. Can I get your address please, as it's not on your website?"

"Of course it isn't stupid. I can't just have everybody seeing where I live. You've got to be discreet, haven't you? You will get my full address when you are here at 7pm. Take this postcode, CM7 3NU."

"CM7 3NU," Colin repeated as he saved the postcode down in his phone.

"Call me when you are at that postcode and then I will give you my door number," said Shereece.

"Thank you Mistress Lilith, I will do," replied Colin ending the call.

"I've got a client coming," said Shereece to Kia as she continued pumping dumbbells. Kia was sitting up in her coffin, now heavily pregnant. "I'll need to do the usual Kia. You know the routine. No noise during my services."

"Yes Shereece," replied Kia. Shereece had been allowing Kia to call her Shereece rather than Mistress Lilith. As time went by, Shereece became less hostile towards Kia.

"Will you ever let me go?" asked Kia in a bold voice. She was now becoming immune to the fear of Shereece, after all she felt her situation couldn't get much worse. Shereece put down her two heavy dumbbells, walked over to Kia and knelt down right beside her. She turned Kia's face to face her.

"You're mine now Kia. You and the baby inside of you are now mine, so get used to it ok?" Kia was now looking at Shereece in disgust. "I'll never let you go, to leave me again like you did all those years. We were together at birth and we will remain together till death," said Shereece as she stroked Kia's hair. "Everything will be ok if you just allow things to be," Shereece continued.

"How can things be ok if!..."

"Shhhhh," Shereece broke Kia's sentence by putting her two fingers to Kia's lips. "Don't fight me Kia, you'll lose. You're only alive because I'm allowing you to be alive. Don't fuck with me. You know what I can do," said Shereece as she continued to stroke Kia's hair. "Just trust me and everything will be alright," whispered Shereece.

"You need help Shereece. Let me out of here and I can get you the help you need," said Kia quietly while looking in Shereece's eyes.

Shereece stopped stroking Kia's hair and just stared at her, then SMACKKK! Shereece firmly slapped Kia across her face.

"My client will be here at 7pm. If you make a sound when he is here I'll kill you," Shereece warned Kia bluntly.

She then calmly got up and exited the basement. Kia lay back down and stared at the basement ceiling. Her face was stinging from the slap. A tear trickled down her cheek, but she forced herself not to burst into tears. 'Not anymore,' Kia thought to herself. 'You've got to be tough now.'

Kia started to look around the basement. 'How can I get out of here? There must be a way,' she thought. But then she remembered Derrick and how Shereece murdered him in his failed attempt to escape.

She began thinking about the baby inside of her, and the life her baby would have being raised by her psychopath sister. "That's not an option," said Kia to herself. 'I've got to get us both out of this,' thought Kia. She started to think of Shereece's client who was coming at 7pm. 'Maybe I should scream and kick in the coffin when they arrive,' thought Kia. She knew Shereece was capable of any threat she gave, but then Kia also knew that she was carrying the child that Shereece proclaimed as her own. 'She wouldn't kill me, not while I'm carrying this child. Fuck it, I'll scream my lungs out. It's my only hope,' thought Kia.

It was now 6.50pm. Shereece had fed Kia and closed her coffin shut after reminding Kia to stay quiet. Shereece's phone began ringing. "Hello," answered Shereece.

"Hi, it's Colin. I'm at the postcode you gave me."

"Ok, are you in a car?"

"Yes, I'm in a blue Audi A3."

"Ok, come out of your car and come to door number 53 on Fiedal Road, the same road you're on."

"Ok." Colin was a short, skinny Turkish man with glasses who was in his thirties. This was his second experience with a dominatrix. Single and lonely, he found the dominatrix experience exciting. Colin walked to door number 53 and pressed the doorbell. He looked above to the camera at the top of the door that was facing down on him. Two minutes went by before Shereece appeared at the door. She opened the door to greet a five foot five timid Colin. Collin was excited but yet intimidated by Shereece's big, bold muscular physique.

"Come in," she said. Colin walked into the house.

"Follow me," said Shereece as she walked Collin through the corridor and across the living room. She then opened the trap door to descend the basement stairs. Colin walked down the stairs quietly behind Shereece and looked around the basement, viewing the chains and coffins on the floor and walls.

"This is some dungeon," he said.

"Shush, no talking until you are spoken to," snapped Shereece.

"Yes Mistress," replied Colin obediently. Shereece took Colin to the middle of the basement. "Money upfront," she said. Colin brought his wallet out from his trouser pocket then handed Shereece £200 after counting it.

"Now undress until you're fully naked," ordered Shereece. Colin obeyed. "Now get on your knees!" said Shereece in a domineering voice while pointing to the floor.

"Yes Mistress," replied Colin.

"It's Mistress Lilith. You will address me as Mistress Lilith," said Shereece.

"Yes Mistress Lilith," replied Colin.

"So, you like to be tied up do you? Well, I've got the perfect thing for you." Shereece disappeared to the rear of the basement, leaving Colin naked on his knees. She reappeared with two long velvet ropes.

"Give me your arms!" She said to Colin. Colin obeyed.

Shereece then proceeded to tie Colin's wrists together tightly behind his back. Once she had tied his wrists together, she went for his ankles and tied them together as tight as she had tied his wrists.

"Now lick my boots," said Shereece as she stuck out her right 9inch foot that was inside of her black leather boot and lifted her heel. Colin licked the side of Shereece's boot and then continued licking to the front.

"That's it my little slave, lick it clean."

"HELP ME! HELP ME! HELP ME!" BOOM! BOOM! Kia screamed and banged from her coffin.

"What the fuck is that?" asked Colin. He couldn't quite make out the words from Kia but he could clearly hear the banging. "It's just a client, it's part of their role play,"

said Shereece.

"What? Nah, I didn't expect to be involved in somebody else's session."

"Just don't worry about it and keep licking," said Shereece. BANG! BANG! BOOM! "HELP ME!" Kia kicked, banged and shouted from her coffin.

"You know what, I want out of this. Untie me now please," said Colin.

"I'll fucking untie you!" shouted Shereece, as she pulled a seven inch Rambo knife from her lower back belt and stabbed Colin in his chest.

"Arrrrrgh," shouted Colin in pain and shock. Shereece then jumped on top of Colin with her legs around his waist and plunged the knife in his chest a second time, then again and again.

"Arrrrgh help me!" screamed Collin as Shereece was stabbing him in a frenzy. Blood was gushing out everywhere as Shereece stabbed away. Her face and leather latex outfit were covered in Colin's blood.

Colin was dead after Shereece plunged a fatal blow into his heart with the knife but even though he was dead, Shereece continued stabbing. She enjoyed the rush she got from stabbing him.

By the time Shereece finally stopped, she had stabbed Collin 46 times. Shereece stood up over Collin's corpse and looked down on the carnage she had caused. She then headed towards Kia's coffin and opened it.

"What have you done?" Kia asked while looking up at Shereece.

"See for yourself," said Shereece. She grabbed Kia's hair and pulled her head up to witness Colin's body, but Kia struggled and tugged her head back, not wanting to see Shereece's horrible work.

"Get off me you evil sick bitch! Get off me!" Kia yelled and struggled, but Shereece was too strong and raised Kia's head and body turning it towards Colin. Kia squeezed her eyes shut.

"Open your eyes. Open your eyes now bitch!" Shereece yelled.

"No get off me!" Kia yelled back. Shereece put the bloody knife she held in her left hand to Kia's right cheek and pressed on to it, piercing Kia's skin.

"Arrrrghh!" Kia yelled and then opened her eyes. "You see? You see what you made me fucking do?" Shereece shouted while gripping Kia's hair. Kia's eyes and mouth opened wide with shock. Seeing Colin's bloodied corpse lying on the basement floor put Kia in total shock.

She looked in disbelief before letting out heart chilling screams. "AAAAAAAHHHH! AHHHHHHH! AAAAAHHHH!"

Shereece then shoved Kia back in the coffin and slammed the coffin lid shut. She then began whistling, picking up Colin's body and bringing it to one of her empty coffins.

After Shereece had put Colin's naked and bloodied body in one of the coffins, she left the basement, went to her kitchen and got a mop, bucket, her favourite strawberry air freshener, a roll of black bin liners and disinfectant. She brought all the items back down to the basement with her and began to clean up Colin's blood.

Shereece was whistling as she mopped away. After cleaning up the blood, she picked up Colin's clothes along with his phone, wallet and shoes that were on the floor. After emptying the wallet, she packed all the items up in one of the black bin liners.

She then took off her own clothes until she was fully naked and added them to the bag. It was time to burn all evidence. 'I'd better clean up first,' Shereece thought to herself. She had been through this routine before on several occasions. She exited the basement and went upstairs to the shower room. Shereece washed herself down thoroughly, scrubbing her skin hard with a bath sponge soaked with shower gel, ridding herself of all of Colin's blood.

After she showered, she got dressed in her room, putting on a black tracksuit along with black Nike air force trainers and a black Nike baseball hat that she dipped low to fully cover her forehead. She then looked at herself in her long wardrobe mirror. "I'm good," she said to herself. Then she went back into the basement to pick up the black bag. She took the bag, went to her kitchen, grabbed a bottle of red wine from her cupboard then exited the house and got into her Ford Mondeo. She knew a park close by where she chose to discard all evidence.

She drove herself to the park that was just five minutes away and parked up in a discrete parking space that was just a minute walk from her destination. Shereece looked around making sure there was nobody in sight before picking up the black bag along with her bottle of red wine before exiting the vehicle. It was now night time and the park was completely empty.

Shereece walked through the park until she got to a remote dark spot that was full of bushes. It was here that she poured some of the red wine on the black bag then set it alight with a lighter she took out of her handbag. Shereece stood there and watched the bag burn along with the clothes and items.

A dark, chilling sensation ran through Shereece's body as she watched the flames. She enjoyed the whole process of killing and discarding of evidence. It made her feel frightened yet in power and ahead of the law. After seeing the bag burn to ashes Shereece headed back to her car. She got in, switched the key in her ignition and turned the car Bluetooth on. She then put David Bowie's song 'Star Man' on loud in her iTunes Store and began driving.

Shereece was a big fan of the song and liked to listen to it after she killed. She drove to her house singing along to the song.

"There's a starrrrrman waiting in the sky he'd like to come and meet us but he thinks he'll blow our minds, there's a starrrrrman waiting in the sky he told us not to blow it cause he knows it's all worthwhile," she sung away.

Arriving back at her house, Shereece parked in her driveway and exited her vehicle. She took the remaining bottle of red wine with her, opened the door to her house and headed straight down to the basement.

She opened Kia's coffin. Kia was awake and the two locked eyes. Shereece sat down on the side of the coffin.

"It looks like I'm going to have to tape your mouth shut on my next session," said Shereece.

"You're not going be able to get away with all this. The people you killed have families. It won't be long before the police track you down here," said Kia.

"They've already been here," said Shereece smiling.

"Who?" blurted Kia.

"The police and detectives." Kia's eyes opened wide.

"They don't know about this basement, and they never will."

"You're delusional," Kia said while shaking her head.

"No I am not."

"God is not going to let you get away with this," said Kia sharply.

"Don't bring God into this. If God was on your side, you wouldn't be here, would you? Be thankful I'm not going to kill you for the stunt you pulled tonight. Now get some rest. You need to just rest and obey me, and if you do, then what happened today won't have to happen again," said Shereece, raising her right eyebrow.

She took a sip of her red wine. "I would offer you some, but we can't have you drinking while carrying my baby, can we Kia?"

Kia stared at Shereece for a moment then looked away. "Goodnight Kia," said Shereece, as she got up and closed the coffin.

Chapter 12

Labour

"Push Kia push!" Shereece said excitedly to Kia. Shereece had taken Kia out of her coffin and put her onto a mattress as soon as Kia went into labour.

Three months had passed since Shereece killed Derrick. Kia was now nine months pregnant and in labour. Kia thought it was a miracle she hadn't miscarried after going through all the hell Shereece had subjected her to, but since Derrick's murder Shereece had kept Kia in a more comfortable condition, by keeping her coffin lid open and constantly being by her side, cleaning her down daily, feeding her, putting a radio on for her and assuring her daily that things will be great between them when raising the child together.

In the beginning, after Shereece killed Derrick, Kia was beyond distressed. She was numb for weeks and stopped responding when Shereece spoke to her. Shereece was lenient in response to Kia's defiance because of her pregnancy. Kia eventually adapted to her situation and began responding to Shereece, fearful of losing the only thing that remained of Derrick. Kia now wanted to have Derrick's baby, but was unsure of what would happen after the child was born.

"I see the head Kia. Come on keep pushing, you're doing great!" said Shereece out loud.

"Awwww! ohhhh!" were the moans of Kia as she desperately tried to push the baby out of her womb. "Ahhhhhh!"

"Come on Kia come on you're almost there!" The baby's head and arms were out of Kia's vagina now.

"Come on Kia keep pushing! Keep pushing!" Shereece shouted while Kia was on the mattress in agony. "Ahhrrrrrrr!" Kia yelled while giving a great forceful push to finally get the baby out.

"It's a girl!" yelled Shereece as the baby slipped into her hands.

"Oh my gosh Kia! It's a girl! it's a girl! I knew it would be. She's so beautiful," said Shereece in joy.

Shereece cut the umbilical cord with a pair of clean, sharp scissors she had bought and saved for this day, then she quickly wrapped the crying baby in a towel and placed her in Kia's arms.

"Look at our baby. She's so beautiful," said Shereece. Kia couldn't help but smile in joy and look at her baby girl. Thoughts of Derrick flashed through her mind while looking at her baby's face. Mixed emotions ran through her. Shereece looked at Kia and said, "Everything is going to be fine. Everything will be perfect now."

"Oh my God Shereece, I'm having pains. Something is wrong. "Oooooowww! ooooowww!" Kia groaned in pain. "There's something inside me Shereece."

Shereece took the newborn baby from Kia and looked down at her vagina. "OH MY GOSH!" Shereece yelled. To her surprise, she saw a baby's head coming out of Kia's vagina. Shereece took the baby from Kia and placed her on the carpet she had prepared.

"They're twins! You've produced twins Kia. For fuck's sake! This is not what I want!" said Shereece out loud in anger. She then began walking in circles in the basement rubbing her head.

"Please Shereece help me deliver this baby!" moaned Kia. Shereece looked at Kia with a stone-cold expression.

She was thinking what to do next. Having twins was not part of her plan. Shereece resented twins because of her own bad experience of having one.

"Please Shereece, help!" Kia cried out. The newborn baby was crying on the floor. So much was going on at once making it hard for Shereece to think straight.

"Fucking hell! The things I do for you Kia," said Shereece as she kneeled on the floor to help deliver the other baby. "Right, push Kia! Push!"

"Arrrrgh!" Kia shouted as she forcefully pushed from her womb. "It hurts! It hurts!" she cried.

"Come on. I've got the head. You're almost there Kia, push!"

"Arrrrrgh," Kia cried out as she pushed hard. The baby slipped right into Shereece's hands.

"I've got her. It's a girl! another girl!" Shereece shouted.

"Waah! Waah!" cried the baby girl. Shereece cut the umbilical cord then stood up holding the baby girl in her arms whilst looking at her face.

"She's so beautiful," Shereece said. Kia looked up at Shereece exhausted, breathing heavily and lost for words. Shereece looked down at Kia with a serious expression on her face. Both the babies were healthy and were now crying.

Shereece glanced at the baby girl on the floor then at Kia.

"This can't work Kia. One of them has to go. I want one child not two. She has to die Kia," said Shereece indicating the baby in her arms.

"No! No! Please no. I'll take care of her Shereece, you won't have to do anything. Please don't kill my baby, please don't!" Kia said hysterically.

"It's the only way this can work Kia," Shereece said while walking with the baby in her arms. "It will be best for both of us. Trust me Kia, I know best."

Shereece knelt down and placed the baby she had in her arms on the basement floor.
She then proceeded to take the scissors she used to cut the umbilical cord out of her gown pocket.

"NO! NO! Please don't!" screamed Kia. Shereece raised the scissors above the baby and pointed the sharp end at the baby's chest.

"It has to be this way Kia."

"NO! Please. Somebody help! Please don't kill my baby!" Kia burst out screaming and crying. She made a desperate attempt to get up but was too weak and exhausted.

Shereece looked at Kia with her fist clenched and her teeth gritted. She then looked at the wiggling baby she had just placed on the floor, and within a flash of a second, WHAAAM! She struck the scissors an inch from the baby's body into the ground.

"Ahhhhhhhh!" Kia screamed, as the scissors lodged into the cement floor. Shereece kneeled upright breathing heavily.

"You're going to fucking take care of her then," Shereece whispered before getting up and exiting the basement. Kia was now crying hysterically.

In no less than four minutes, Shereece came back into the basement with a blanket. She picked up baby number 2 from the floor and held her in the blanket.

"I'm sorry for losing my temper Kia. I know I have anger issues," said Shereece laughing at the same time.

"We'll take care of both our babies, but you've got to work with me Kia."

"Ye, ye, yes," stuttered Kia.

"What should we name them?" Shereece asked.

"I, I don't know yet," Kia answered with a tear dripping down her cheek. Shereece stared at the baby in her arms and said, "We'll name her Shyla."

She then looked at the baby on the floor lying on the blanket and said, "We'll name her Peree. Shyla and Peree. How about that Kia?" Shereece now had a big smile on her face and handed Kia her child.

"They're nice names. Yeah we can go with them," said Kia.

"They're beautiful, aren't they Kia?"

"Yes, yes they are." Kia muttered. Kia was very scared of saying anything wrong and had learned from spending time as a prisoner of Shereece that it was better to abide by Shereece's rules and not say anything to make Shereece's temper flare. But she was so confused now, she had two babies to think of.

How was she going to raise them trapped in captivity? How? How could she maintain their safety knowing the lunatic Shereece was, a cold-hearted killer who was prepared to kill a baby? 'Somebody has to find me,' Kia thought to herself. 'My friends and Derrick's family will all be looking for me now, along with my work colleagues.'

The problem was, Kia never revealed to her friends that she was going to visit her sister, neither did Derrick. Kia was very private about her sister and told Derrick to keep the visit private. But as odd as her sister had been growing up, never in a million years did Kia think this all could take place. Kia's wrists were cuffed together, but her legs were loose. She wouldn't dare at this time attempt to physically challenge Shereece. She was too weak from having the babies and knew Shereece would easily overpower her.

"I've saved up enough money from my work as a dominatrix to support us all for now. We're just going to take it one day at a time Kia, is that understood?" said Shereece.

"Yes it's understood," Kia replied. Shereece had a green baby bathtub she had previously brought down to the basement, and began to bathe Shyla. After finishing Shyla's bath, she passed Shyla to Kia and Kia sat up and began breastfeeding her. Shereece then bathed Peree in the baby bath.

"Do you think you can breast feed both of them?" asked Shereece.

"Not with my hands cuffed. Can you uncuff me Shereece? Just to feed them?" asked Kia.

"I'm afraid I can't Kia. Don't worry I'll take care of Peree," said Shereece. She put crying Peree on the carpet and headed out the basement and to the kitchen. She prepared baby milk in a bottle for Peree then went back down to the basement.

"Don't cry Peree, don't cry. Mummy is here," said Shereece as she picked up Peree. She put the bottle's teat in Peree's mouth and Peree instantly began sucking.

"Aww that's my baby girl," said Shereece looking down at Peree and smiling. "How are you doing over there with Shyla?" asked Shereece.

"She's feeding well," said Kia smiling.

"Good, good," said Shereece still smiling. "I'm gonna buy you everything you need my little pumpkin," said Shereece to Peree.

"Where will they sleep?" asked Kia.

"I bought a cot. It's in my bedroom. They both will sleep in there."

"Can you bring the cot down here please Shereece? You did say we will raise them together. I want to be as close to our babies as possible. You're going to need the help Shereece. You need to trust me and uncuff my wrists. I want to raise our babies with you. I no longer want to leave.

Trust me Shereece. You can trust me. You said you've saved up enough money to support us for now, so you no longer need to work down here. There's enough space down here for us to nurture them," said Kia.

Shereece went silent as her brain went into thought mode. She finished feeding Peree, laid her on the carpet and got up.

"I'll bring the cot down," said Shereece, then she exited the basement.

The very next morning Kia woke up to two crying babies. Shereece had brought down the cot along with a mattress and blankets for herself the night before. She had placed Shyla and Peree both in the cot overnight. Shereece had also been seeing to the babies when they needed feeding through the night by making them bottles. Kia spent the night in her coffin cuffed and shackled. Shereece opened Kia's coffin.

"Morning Kia," said Shereece.

"Morning Shereece," replied Kia.

"You need to help me with these babies, I've got things to do," Shereece told Kia.

"That's fine I can do that."

"I'm going to go shopping. There are things I need to buy. Feed and take care of them before I get back. I've made them bottles, or you can breast feed them, it's up to you."

"I'll breastfeed them."

"Ok." Then to Kia's amazement, Shereece uncuffed her wrists. It felt so good for Kia to be uncuffed after such a long time. Her wrists had bright red lines round them and were sore. Kia bent her hands back and forth.

"Can I trust you?" asked Shereece,

"Yes you can trust me," Kia assured her.

"Okay, sit up," said Shereece as she helped Kia up.

"What about my ankles?" Kia asked, pointing to her ankles which were still shackled.

"Don't ask me anymore questions Kia, just look after our babies until I get back." Shereece picked Peree and Shyla up from the cot. Kia pulled up her shirt to prepare for breastfeeding them. Shereece just about managed to hand them both down to Kia. Kia began to breast feed them both with the assistance of Shereece.

"It's going to be hard for you to manage them both Kia. I'll feed Peree by the bottle while you breastfeed Shyla."

"Ok thank you." Shereece took Peree and fed her by the bottle. When Shereece finished feeding Peree, she put her in her cot.

"I'm going now Kia. Do you want me to put Shyla in her bed?" asked Shereece,

"No it's fine I've got her."

"Ok, well I'll see you soon," said Shereece before exiting the basement. Kia heard several locks to the basement trap door click.

Shereece went to her bedroom and put a pillow on her stomach, then tied a skipping rope around her waist to strap the pillow to her belly. She knew eventually she would be taking the babies out, and wanted people to think that she was pregnant, so that it wouldn't be a surprise when people saw her with Kia's twins.

She had been dressing like this whenever she left the house for the past six months. Shereece then left the house, headed to Bluendale shopping centre and went to Argos. She was shopping for a pram for the twin babies.

In the Argos store, Shereece bumped into her next door neighbour Catherine, a short white woman in her fifties who had lived next to her for the past five years. "Hey Catherine, how are you?" asked Shereece as she hugged Catherine's slim frame.

"I'm fine," Catherine replied as she adjusted the glasses on her face, "and you?"

"I'm great."

"Your stomach is getting so big now."

"Yeah I'm due any moment now."

"Awww, do you know what you're having?"

"Yes they're girls."

"They're? What you mean they're?"

"I'm having twins," said Shereece smiling with joy.

"Shut up! No way!" said Catherine in a shocked manner. "Wow Shereece that's so amazing. I cannot believe it. I can't wait to see them. Can I have a feel?" said Catherine, in reference to feeling Sheerece's stomach. Shereece's heart started beating fast.

"Oh no please don't, I'm having stomach pains at the minute and I really get uncomfortable when people touch my tummy," said Shereece. Then she looked at her watch.

I'm running late Catherine. I'll see you soon," said Shereece as she walked away.

Meanwhile Kia was at home uncuffed with Shyla in her arms. Shyla was asleep. Kia started thinking of ways to escape, but she knew the trap door of the basement was locked, and besides that, her ankles were shackled. Kia managed to lay Shyla on the floor without hurting her, then she hurled herself out of the wooden coffin with her hands.

She tried to stand up but was too weak to get on her feet. So she began to get on her knees and crawl. She started to crawl towards the basement stairs that lead to the trap door. She got to the stairs and managed to get up a step by dragging herself up with her arms.

Still exhausted from having the twins, she knew she would be too weak to drag herself to the top of the stairs. Kia slumped back down the step and lay on the floor.

After a minute she got back on her hands and knees and began crawling round the massive basement. She was looking for a weapon to attack Shereece with. She stumbled across a red metal box next to one of Shereece's dominatrix apparatus. The box had a lock on it but was unlocked. Kia opened the box. Inside was a book titled 'Satanic worship'.

"Oh my God," said Shereece. Then she heard footsteps from the basement ceiling. Kia dropped the book and crawled as fast as she could back to her coffin. The basement trap door began to unlock. Kia threw herself in her coffin quickly. Shereece started descending the basement stairs.

"Hi Kia," said Shereece with her right hand clenched to a shopping bag. "I brought you some Chinese takeaway. Why is Shyla on the floor Kia?"

"My arms got really tired. I had to put her down."

"Come here honey," said Shereece as she picked up Shyla, cradled her in her arms before putting her in her cot. Shereece then went into her bag and handed Kia a box of Chinese special fried rice along with a plastic fork. "I know you must be hungry Kia."

"Yes I am, thank you," said Kia as she took the food. Shereece sat down on a chair beside Kia's coffin and began to eat from her own box of special fried rice.

"I bought our babies a pram today Kia. It's lovely. I'll bring it down for you to see in a bit," Shereece said while chewing on her food.

"Ok," replied Kia sadly acknowledging that it would be Shereece spending time with her babies outside and not her.

"I've been meaning to tell you something Kia," Shereece blurted out.

"What is it Shereece?"

"Let's finish eating, then I'll let you know." When Shereece finished her food, she looked at Kia and said, "I worship the Devil Kia. I worship Satan, and I want you to join my religion."

Kia stared at Shereece stone faced, thinking about the book she had seen in the box.

"Why do you worship Satan Shereece?"

"Because Satan is who I'm inclined with. Everything about me coincides with Satan not with God. I like to torture. I like to kill. I love orgies. I'm greedy, and I don't deny any of this. Satan rewards me in many ways as long as I keep up my sacrifices. I make human sacrifices to please my lord Satan who keeps me ahead of the law and will make my business and everything I venture in thrive. Satan is real and will reward you too if you join the religion," said Shereece.

"How many people have you killed?" asked Kia.

"Many. Loads, and I'll keep on killing and killing and keep on getting away with it, because my Lord Satan will not allow me to get caught. I have followers under me. A few of my submissive slaves that do anything I ask of them. They too are now committed to my satanic religion. I'll soon introduce you to them, but I want you to have faith in the religion first."

"I'm a Christian Shereece, and I plan on staying one."

"Listen to me Kia, joining my religion is the only way I can trust you, and if I can trust you, I can set you free. Once you commit to Satan through my rituals, I'll know you won't leave me, then we can run our little family properly. I won't need to keep you in a coffin anymore. Just think about it Kia, have a good long think about it. Satan needs more worshippers, and I've pledged to bring him more followers."

"Ok, I'll think about it," said Kia.

Kia had no real intention of joining the Anti-Christ religion, but was scared of directly refusing Shereece, and the thought of Shereece setting her free had enticed Kia into agreeing to think about joining Shereece's cult.

Chapter 13

The Cult

"Wake up Kia!" Kia was woken up by Shereece talking loudly. It was 8 o'clock in the morning. Kia could hear the babies crying from their cot. "I've changed them already, they just need feeding now," said Shereece.

Shereece uncuffed Kia, helped sit her up, then picked up Peree and put her in Kia's arms. "Breastfeed her while I feed Shyla by the bottle," said Shereece. She then picked up Shyla and began feeding her from a bottle she had already prepared. "I've got some guests coming round later. I'd like you to meet them," said Shereece while sitting on her chair feeding Shyla.

"Why do you want me to meet them Shereece?"

"Because they're part of my cult, so they are considered part of this family." Kia's heart began to race.

'What type of sick individuals is Shereece going to introduce me to?' Kia thought to herself.

"Shereece, maybe you should give it a bit more time before introducing me to your friends."

"Stop!" Shereece shouted out before Kia could say another word. "They're not my friends. I don't do friends. They're my submissives, and I've decided you will see them today, is that understood?"

"Ok Shereece whatever you say," said Kia with annoyance in her tone.

"Is that an attitude I hear coming from you Kia?"

"No it's not. I'll meet your friends," said Kia under her breath.

At 7 o'clock in that evening there was a ring on Shereece's door bell. Shereece was in her basement when the doorbell rang.

"That must be them," Shereece said. She looked at her security camera to see who it was at the door and saw that it was who she was expecting. Shereece left the basement to go and answer the door. She got to the door and opened it fully.

"Good evening my slaves," Shereece said to the two men standing on her doorstep. Both men were white. One of them was named Ricky. Ricky was forty years old and was tall, standing at six feet one. He had a slim build, bald head and a short salt and pepper beard that connected to his moustache.

The other man was named Victor. He was five foot seven and had a chubby physique. He wore glasses and had a stubble of a brown beard and a moustache, along with short curly brown hair.

Both men were Shereece's obedient slaves. They started off as her clients, but through time Shereece had groomed them into joining her Satanic worship religion, and being on call for her every demand 24/7. Both men were more than happy to serve Shereece. She knew how to pick her slaves and had spotted insecurities to manipulate in both men.

"Come in," said Shereece to her two slaves.

"Yes Mistress Lilith," they both replied as they walked into the house. Shereece walked down to her basement and they followed her down.

Once in the basement they continued to follow Shereece, stopping when she stopped and walking when she did. They walked past Kia's closed coffin and the babies in their cot.

Neither Ricky nor Victor glanced at the babies. They didn't take their eyes off Shereece.

"Get on your knees," said Shereece. Both of her slaves obeyed. "Kiss my feet, both of you," said Shereece sternly.

Ricky and Victor obeyed her command and kissed one foot each. "Good boys," said Shereece. She then got her black wooden chair and sat down in front of her two slaves.

"Now I'd like you both to meet a new member of this family. My twin sister Kia. Come on over," said Shereece.

Her two slaves followed by crawling behind her on their hands and knees. Shereece got to Kia's coffin and opened it. Kia was asleep.

"Stand up boys," said Shereece. Both men stood up.

"Wake up Kia, wake up. There's people I want you to meet," said Shereece as she tapped Kia a few times on her right cheek, waking her up in the process. Kia opened her eyes widely. She saw all three individuals standing above her.

"Wakey wakey Kia. I hope you slept well, but it's time to wake up. Here is Ricky," Shereece said as she put her right hand on Ricky's left shoulder, "and here is Victor," she said, as she put her left hand on Victor's right shoulder. "These are both my subs I was telling you about. They obey me, and they're going to help us out with this family. Ricky, Vic, both of you say hello to Kia,"

Shereece instructed the slaves as she snapped her fingers. "Hello Kia," said Ricky and Victor simultaneously. It was like they were robots the way they obeyed Shereece and answered her at the same time.

"Hel..... Hello," Kia stuttered. "Nice to meet you both. How are the babies?" Kia asked Shereece changing the subject.

"They are fine. Both are fast asleep," said Shereece.

"Well now you've met my slaves, would you like to join us for our evening ritual? We will be praying to our Lord Satan. You can learn our rituals and practice with us," Shereece continued.

"No thank you," said Kia politely.

"Kia if you're going to be a part of this family, you're going to have to follow our beliefs and that means participating in our rituals."

"I'm a Christian Shereece. Please, don't make me convert to anything else. I know nothing about your religion, and I'm confident in my own beliefs. Christianity," said Kia. Shereece looked at her two subs, then back down at Kia.

"You're going to have to come round Kia. Tonight you can just watch us but soon you're going to have to join us," said Shereece. Shereece made Kia sit up.

"Come slaves. It's time," said Shereece as she clicked her fingers. She walked into the middle of the basement with her slaves crawling after her.

When she stopped she told her subs to kneel. She then walked to the right side of the basement that had a chest of drawers. She opened one of the drawers and brought out a set of candles and candle holders. She put the candles in the holders then started placing the candles around them and herself until they were all surrounded by candles. She then began to light them one by one.

There was already some light in the basement as Shereece always left one of the ceiling light bulbs on, but the candles made the basement extra bright. Shereece got on her knees and began to recite the words "Hail Satan". Kia was watching it all from her coffin, frightened and uncomfortable.

"My servants, it is time for you both to fully commit to our lord and make a human sacrifice for him. As you both know, I now have two babies to raise. They are the two most important things to me now and I cannot let anything in this world hinder me from raising them. It wasn't in my plans to have two children, but fate has made things be this way. So I accept it as my calling to raise two girls.

The human sacrifice we will make for our Lord Satan will secure my protection from the law, stop anyone from taking my babies, and bring me all the financial wealth I need. In turn I will reward both of you with mind blowing sex that you can only dream of. I'll make your fantasies a reality, and your faith in me and Satan will make your day to day lives sweeter than you can imagine. Will you both commit to this human sacrifice for me and Satan?" asked Shereece.

"Yes Mistress Lilith," replied Ricky and Victor sincerely.

"Good. It must be a woman, In Satan's bible, it says a female sacrifice will bring protection from outsiders. I need protection from the law. I've had police on my back already. I cannot have them catch me for anything I've done or anything I will do. We will find us a woman tonight, and sacrifice her right here in this basement," said Shereece.

Ricky and Victor had never killed before but were aware of Shereece's murders.

"How will we find our sacrifice?" asked Ricky.

"Just follow my instructions and we will have her tonight," said Shereece.

At 11pm that same night Shereece was in a car with Ricky and Victor. Ricky was driving his blue Ford Escort with Shereece in the passenger seat and Victor in the back. Shereece had closed Kia's coffin. She had also changed and fed both the babies before she left the house. She had told Ricky to drive her to a lesbian nightclub called the Triangle.

"I'll find my victim in here for sure. So many thirsty lesbians in this club. I used to pick up women there when I was on my lesbo flow all the time," Shereece told them as she brushed down her hair.

"Can I ask a personal question Mistress?" asked Ricky.

"Go on," replied Shereece.

"Who do you prefer sexually, men or women?"

"It depends what mood I'm in....It really just depends what mood I'm in. Right now, I fancy me a woman............to kill." said Shereece.

They were almost at the Triangle night club but were circling around an estate close to the club to find a parking space.

"Pull up there on that side road," said Shereece as she pointed to an empty parking space she saw. Ricky parked in the space Shereece had pointed at.

"Right, you two are going to wait here for me until I get back. Anyone I bring out might find it awkward and intimidating with you both being in the car. I only brought you with me in case I fail to bring a woman back out of the club. If I am not able to lure a woman into the car from the club, then both of you are going to kidnap a woman off the street and force her into the boot. Hopefully we won't need to do it that way as that's more hard work, but if it comes to that you're both down right?" Shereece checked.

"Yes Mistress," replied Ricky and Victor.

"If I do get our sacrifice to get into the car with us, you're both going to make out that you're my brothers and have come to pick me up because I can't drive. That's the story you both go along with if she happens to ask you any questions."

"Ok Mistress," replied Victor and Ricky.

"Alright, here I go," said Shereece as she fixed her lipstick in the car mirror above her. She exited the vehicle and walked round the corner then towards the Triangle nightclub. There was a lengthy queue outside of the club. Shereece queued up behind two ladies who were at the back of the line. Fifteen minutes passed before Shereece finally got to the nightclub door.

"Can I look in your bag please?" the tall, broad, black doorman asked Shereece.

"No problem," Shereece responded as she opened her bag to be checked. The door man flashed a torch through Shereece's bag as he peered in.

"Ok, that's cool. Now can I see some ID?" Shereece delved into her bag and pulled out her driver's licence and handed it to the doorman. The doorman glanced at the licence then looked at Shereece. There was a scanner beside the doorman.

"Run your ID under the scanner until it takes a photo," said the doorman as he gave her back her driver's licence. Shereece did as he said. "Ok you're good. Go through the door please." Shereece walked through the door and faced a counter as soon as she got in.

"Twenty pounds please," said the blonde-haired woman behind the counter. Shereece dug into her bag and pulled out a twenty-pound note. She gave it to the lady behind the counter, then held out her hand. The lady behind the counter stamped Shereece's hand with an illuminous marker to show she had paid to get in.

Shereece then walked into the club. It was a while since she had last been here. The club was packed with house music playing in the background. Shereece had a black fur jacket on, along with a black PVC dress on underneath. She spotted a petite, young white woman who looked to be in her mid-twenties, dressed in red, dancing alone in the left side corner of the club. Shereece approached her.

"Hey how are you?" Shereece asked in a friendly manner.

"Sorry, what's that?" replied the woman still dancing.

"How are you?!" Shereece repeated, much louder this time to be heard above the sound of the music.

"I'm fine!" said the woman loud enough for Shereece to hear her.

"My name is Shereece, what's yours?"

"I'm Daisy!"

"Nice to meet you Daisy," Shereece replied as she put out her hand for Daisy to shake.

"I'm sorry I can't shake your hand!"

"Oh, why is that?"

"Because she's my girlfriend!" replied a voice that came from behind Shereece.

Shereece turned around to face the person behind her. When she did, she saw in front of her a six -foot tall, butch looking, black woman with short black hair who looked to be in her early thirties, holding two glasses of whisky and coke.

"Can you move away from my girlfriend please? NOW!" said the butch looking lady, loudly and sternly.

"My bad," said Shereece, embarrassed as she walked away from both the women. She then started to walk through the crowd towards the cloakroom and paid two pounds to hang up her fur jacket.

Then she started walking through the crowd again, trying to spot a lady who was on her own. Her eyes fell on a white, short, five-foot four woman with short red hair who was dancing on her own near the nightclub bar.

Shereece approached the woman. When she got to the redhead, she introduced herself. "Hi! My name is Shereece! What's yours?!"

"I'm Kelly!" replied the redhead. Not wanting to make the same mistake again, Shereece asked, "Do you have a partner Kelly?"

"No I don't, in fact I'm here alone."

'Perfect,' thought Shereece. "I'm here on my own too," Shereece told Kelly.

"Wow. Well nice to meet you Shereece," said Kelly as she put her hand out. Shereece shook Kelly's hand, then raised it to her mouth and kissed it.

"Awww you're sweet," said Kelly smiling.

"So, what's a pretty thing like you doing single and out alone?" Shereece asked.

"I'm just enjoying my single life and letting my hair down. What about you, are you single?"

"Well, I wouldn't be talking to you if I wasn't."

"Ahhh, that's what they all say."

"Nah not me. I'm a faithful woman through and through."

"Ok."

"So, can I get you a drink?"

"Yeah you can," replied Kelly confidently.

"What you having?"

"I'll have a vodka and coke." Shereece waved to the bartender. The female bartender came over to Shereece.

"Hi, what can I get you?" asked the bartender.

"Can I get two shots of vodka with coke, and a Diet Coke please?" said Shereece as she leaned over the bar.

"No problem," said the bartender. The bartender prepared both the drinks and then handed them to Shereece. Shereece passed the vodka and coke glass to Kelly.

"Thank you. So, where you from?" asked Kelly after taking a sip of her drink.

"As in background or where I live?" replied Shereece leaning towards Kelly so she wouldn't have to speak so loudly. Shereece took a whiff in of Kelly's perfume and liked the smell.

"Where do you live I mean?" asked Kelly leaning her right elbow on the bar.

"I live in Bluendale, born and raised." Shereece didn't hesitate to give out her genuine information as she was planning on killing Kelly anyway.

"Oh yeah? So you're not far from here then."

"No, I'm not. What about you? Where you from?"

"I'm from Chelmsford."

"Chelmsford is just up the road. You're not far from here either?"

"No I'm not," Kelly confirmed before asking, "do you smoke?"

"Just cigarettes here and there."

"Come, let's go to the smoking area outside, I wanna have a cigarette." Kelly took hold of Shereece's wrist and pulled her along with her to the smoking area.

Kelly went into her purse and took out a box of sovereign dual cigarettes. She took out two cigarettes and handed one to Shereece, then put the other one in between her lips. She then took out a lighter and lit her cigarette up. Shereece put the cigarette

Kelly gave her in between her lips and leaned forward towards Kelly, indicating for Kelly to light it and she obliged. They both started to take drags from the cigarettes.

"You are so toned up and muscular, you must live in a gym," said Kelly, looking at Shereece's frame.

"Actually, I mostly work out at home." Kelly stroked Shereece's left arm squeezing her bicep in the process.

"I think you're well, sexy," said Kelly looking Shereece's arm up and down, liking what she saw.

"You're not too bad yourself."

"I've never dated a woman with a figure like yours before."

"How old are you Kelly?"

"I'm twenty-three, and you?"

"I'm whatever age you want me to be honey," said Shereece as she smiled. Kelly smiled and was about to speak but Shereece cut her off by saying "shhhhhh." Shereece then leaned towards Kelly's face and kissed Kelly who closed her eyes and began to passionately return Shereece's kiss.

It was 3am when Ricky pulled up outside of Shereece's house. Victor was in the passenger seat and Shereece and Kelly were in the back of the car.

Shereece had persuaded Kelly to come home with her after buying her many shots of vodka. Kelly was now tipsy and half asleep in the backseat. Shereece had told Kelly that Ricky and Victor were her half-brothers and had come to pick her up after having a night out themselves.

Kelly was tipsy enough to believe anything at this point. She was a light-weight drinker and generally couldn't handle her drink very well.

"Wakey wakey," Shereece said to Kelly as she shook her arm. "We're here."

Kelly opened both her eyes fully. Shereece took Kelly by her left wrist and helped her out of the car. Ricky and Victor also came out of the car. Shereece started walking Kelly towards the front door of her house. Kelly was walking awkwardly from being tipsy but turned around and noticed Ricky and Victor were walking behind them.

"Where are they going? I thought they were just dropping us off," said Kelly.

"Oh, I'm just going to give them a drink before they head off. I haven't seen them in a while and I think it would be polite to let them in for a bit before they go," said Shereece.

"I....I don't know about this. Maybe I should just go home," said Kelly.

"No don't be silly. They're just my brothers. They'll be gone in ten minutes I promise, then it will be just me and you," said Shereece convincingly.

"Well..... ok I guess," said Kelly. Shereece took her door key out of her handbag and opened her front door. She led Kelly in by her hand and Ricky and Victor followed them. Shereece then double locked the door behind them before they all walked into the living room.

"Sit down babes," said Shereece as she placed Kelly down on her living room sofa. Ricky and Victor quietly sat on the sofas opposite Kelly.

"So who's having what? I've got Hennessy and Courvoisier," said Shereece.

"I'm ok. I think I've had enough to drink," said Kelly.

"Oh come on Kelly, I'm not just going to have a glass with my brothers." Shereece was planning to slip one of her date rape drugs into Kelly's drink.

"I'll have a glass of Hennessy and coke," said Ricky.

"Make that two," said Victor.

"I'll pour you a Hennessy and coke Kelly," said Shereece. Kelly stayed quiet while Shereece went into the kitchen to make the drinks. Kelly looked at Ricky and Victor. They both were staring at Kelly with stone cold expressions on their faces.

"You two don't talk much, do you?" said Kelly. Ricky and Victor stayed quiet. "So how was your night out?" asked Kelly. Ricky and Victor remained silent.

"Ok, I'm gonna leave," said Kelly feeling uncomfortable. She got up from the sofa and headed towards the front door.

"Where are you going?!" Ricky shouted as he went after Kelly. Kelly ran to the front door and tried to open it by pushing down the handle, but it was locked. Ricky grabbed Kelly around the neck with his arm.

"Get off me! HELP!" screamed Kelly as she tried to free herself from Ricky's arm. Victor got up to assist Ricky. Hearing the commotion, Shereece came out of the kitchen.

"What's going on?" asked Shereece.

"She's trying to escape!" said Victor.

"Get the fuck off me! Help!" screamed Kelly. Shereece ran up to Kelly and grabbed her by the hair away from Ricky.

"Shereece, what are you doing?!" screamed Kelly in horror and confusion. Shereece put her right arm round Kelly's neck placing her in a headlock position.

"Shereece please let me go, let me go!" screamed Kelly as loud as she could. Shereece used her left hand to cover Kelly's mouth. Kelly struggled hard to free herself from Shereece until they both fell to ground. Shereece squeezed her right arm that was still locked around Kelly's neck as hard as she could, then SNAP! Shereece gave an enormous tug on Kelly's neck so hard that she broke it.

Shereece then got up and stood over Kelly's lifeless body. She then looked over to Ricky and Victor who we're now standing in front of her.

"Pick her up and bring her down to the basement," said Shereece sternly.

"Yes Mistress," they both replied.

Shereece led the way to the trap door and opened it. They all entered the basement. Shereece walked past the sleeping babies, checking on them as she headed to the middle of the basement.

"Lay her here," Shereece said pointing to the ground in front of her. Ricky and Victor obeyed.

"What happened? Why did she try to run away?" asked Shereece.

"She just started asking questions, then she got up and ran for the door," said Victor.

"Questions like what? You twats should have kept her entertained. People could have heard all of that commotion," said Shereece angrily.

"Sorry Mistress," said Victor.

"Sorry Mistress," said Ricky.

"Idiots!" said Shereece as she walked off. Shereece returned less than two minutes later with a bag full of candles and candle holders in her left hand. In her right hand was a seven- inch sharp steak knife clenched tight in her fist.

"We've got to cut her heart out. In order to make the sacrifice, the heart must be removed and prayed on," said Shereece. Ricky and Victor both stood in silence.

"Are you both with me on this?" asked Shereece.

"Yes I am Mistress, I'm with you all the way," said Ricky. Shereece turned her face to Victor as if to get his clarification too.

"Yes Mistress, I am with you fully," said Victor.

"Good," said Shereece.

She then got on her knees and began cutting Kelly's clothes off her body and dragging until Kelly was fully naked.

"Help me spread her body into a star shape," said Shereece.

Ricky got down on his knees and spread Kelly's legs apart as far as he could. Shereece put down her knife and bag of candles before spreading Kelly's arms as far apart from Kelly's body as she could.

Kelly's body was now almost in a star shape. Shereece then dug into her bag of candles and took the candles out along with the candle holders.

After putting the candles in the holders, she started to walk around Kelly's corpse placing candles around Kelly's body, lighting them as she went along, until Kelly's body was surrounded by lit candles. Shereece then turned the basement light off.

The lit candles brightened the basement up more than enough for Shereece to see what she was doing.

"Both of you get on your knees," said Shereece to Ricky and Victor. Ricky and Victor obeyed Shereece and got on their knees.

Shereece picked up her knife and sat on Kelly's stomach. WHAM! She then plunged her knife into the left side of Kelly's chest and sliced down until there was a massive gash in Kelly's breast, big enough for Shereece to see Kelly's heart. Shereece plunged her hand into Kelly's now ripped open, bloodied chest, pulled apart Kelly's chest plate, and ripped her heart out. Blood splatted out over Kelly's and Shereece's body.

Victor squeezed his eyes shut and turned his face from the bloody scene. But Ricky stayed staring at the whole ritual, fixated on everything that was occurring. Shereece held Kelly's heart in her right hand high in the air. Blood was trickling down Shereece's arm.

"I want you both to repeat after me," demanded Shereece.

"Dear Satan, accept this sacrifice as a tribute to you. In return, give us protection from outsiders, prosperity, and a beautiful eternal life in your kingdom after death." Victor and Ricky repeated Shereece's words one after the other.

"Hail Satan!" said Shereece out loud.

"Hail Satan!" Victor and Ricky repeated.

Shereece picked her knife up from beside her and sliced Kelly's heart open before squeezing the heart over her face and head.

Shereece's face was dripping with Kelly's blood. Shereece turned to Ricky and Victor and squeezed blood from Kelly's heart over both their heads. Blood poured down their faces. Ricky stuck his tongue out, collecting some of Kelly's blood in his mouth. Shereece smiled while watching Ricky drink Kelly's blood.

"I'm going to store her!" Shereece said out loud in excitement. She headed towards one of her several coffins stored in the basement wall and dragged it out.

After putting the coffin beside Kelly's body, she ordered Ricky and Victor to put the body in along with the heart. After putting Kelly's body in the coffin, they all lifted it and put it back in the wall.

"Both of you get naked now, your clothes are covered in blood. I'm going to wash them, then you're both going home," said Shereece.

"Yes Mistress, replied Ricky and Victor.
Ricky and Victor took all their clothes off and gave them to Shereece who then headed back up into the kitchen to the washing machine.

After putting the clothes on a hot wash cycle, Shereece took a seat in the kitchen and watched the machine spin. She sat there filled with excitement and anxiety at the same time. She was happy with killing Kelly and performing her satanic sacrifice. But she was also a little bit worried that she might not get away with the murder. 'I've got to clean up, and so have they,' Shereece thought to herself. She headed back down to the basement.

"Both of you need to shower," she said to Ricky and Victor. "Come with me both of you."

They followed her out of the basement to the bathroom. Shereece turned the shower on and turned the temperature to the hot level.

"Get in Ricky," she ordered. Ricky got into the shower. Shereece handed Ricky a bottle of Lynx shower gel and a bath scrub.

"Clean yourself up thoroughly," said Shereece.

One by one they all took turns in the shower, scrubbing themselves clean. With the showers complete Shereece took Ricky and Victor to the living room while she went into the basement with a mop, bucket and bleach to clean up all the blood.

As Shereece was mopping up the blood, she started thinking about what her human sacrifice to Satan would bring her in life. She strongly believed it would keep her from getting caught for her crimes, and bring her a man that loved her. She now had her babies, although she only wanted one child, she was now content with the two. But she knew it would be difficult raising them both alone.

Shereece wanted a full family. 'A husband will complete me, a husband like Derrick, good looking, successful and fully devoted to me, she thought.' Shereece finished mopping up all the blood then headed out of the basement.

Coming into the living room, she saw that Victor and Ricky were fast asleep on her sofa. Knowing that their clothes still needed to wash and dry, she left them both to sleep. She took the mop and bucket up to her bathroom and cleaned it out thoroughly. She then headed back downstairs to the kitchen.

The washing machine was bleeping, signalling that the wash was complete. Shereece took the clothes out and transferred them to her tumble dryer that was right beside the washing machine. She turned the dryer on, sat on one of her kitchen chairs and watched the clothes dry.

Forty-five minutes went by before the tumble dryer started bleeping on completion. The clothes were dry. Shereece took the clothes out of the tumble dryer, walked into the living room with them and dropped them on the couch beside Victor. Shereece snapped her fingers twice.

"Wake up! she said, loud enough for Ricky and Victor to hear her. They both woke up. "Get dressed, your clothes are ready," she said pointing at the clothes.

Ricky and Victor got up and started getting dressed. "I'm proud of you both for following through tonight with the sacrifice. You will both be rewarded, but not this morning."

"Can I have the pleasure of licking your feet Mistress?" asked Victor.

"Not now. Now you both go home and get some rest, and not a word of what happened tonight to anyone....ANYONE!" Shereece stressed.

"Yes Mistress Lilith," they both replied. Ricky and Victor left the house quietly and Shereece closed the door behind them.

Shereece woke up at 9am to Shyla and Peree crying. She opened Kia's coffin and woke her up.

"The babies need feeding. I want you to help me," she said to Kia.

"Yes that's fine," Kia said, yawning and struggling to lean up.

"What happened here last night? I heard some commotion. Is everything ok?" asked Kia.

"Everything is good as gold. The babies slept well. I was just doing some cleaning. Anyway, I'm going to go and get their bottles made, then you can help me feed them."

"Bottles? Why Shereece? I can breastfeed them."

"And I just get to sit and watch?" said Shereece sarcastically.

"What's the problem Shereece?"

"The problem is I would like to feed them too. They're my babies too, and we can't just keep switching from breast milk to bottle milk. I've decided we're just going to stick to feeding them by the bottle from now on."

"Ok," said Kia, upset but nodding her head in agreement.

"Good. Now let me go and get their bottles."

"They're going to need to be bathed and changed too," said Kia. Shereece looked Kia dead in her eyes.

"You don't think I know that?! These aren't the first babies I've cared for you know! What do you think I was doing as a nursery teacher, sitting on my arse?!" Shereece said sarcastically. Kia could see she had angered Shereece.

"I'm, I'm sorry Shereece. Of course you know what you're doing," a frightened Kia replied.

"Now relax while I make their bottles."

Shereece went to the kitchen and made two baby bottles of milk, then brought them down to the basement. She uncuffed Kia then went to the babies' cot.

"Aww don't cry baby, mummy is here," said Shereece as she picked up Shyla and handed her to Kia and then gave Kia one of the milk bottles. She then went back to the cot and picked up Peree.

"Hey baby no crying for mummy ok?" she said to Peree before putting the milk bottle teat in Peree's mouth. Both the babies went quiet as they drank the milk from the bottles. After Shereece and Kia fed the babies, Shereece bathed them.

Two weeks went by. Shereece had been taking care of the babies, bathing them, changing them, and feeding them with a little help from Kia who was still bound in her coffin.

Shereece only released Kia's handcuffs to help feed and nurture the babies, but she kept her ankles shackled. She had been shopping, buying baby clothes, nappies, milk and wipes. Making sure she had all the necessities for Shyla and Peree.

Apart from taking care of the babies, Shereece now had her mind set on finding her dream man. She made a profile on a dating app called 'matchup' from her iPhone which read: *Better than your average. Fun loving and spontaneous woman seeking a serious relationship with a man who knows how to treat a lady. I'm a perfectionist and won't take anything less than my standards require.*

Shereece added her name, age, and a picture showing the side of her face and body wearing a skintight dress.

Sitting in her living room on her sofa, after putting the babies to sleep, Shereece began flicking through the matchup dating app. Pressing the 'like' option button on men she was attracted to.

After flicking through for ten minutes, she eventually matched up with a handsome black guy whose profile name was Freddy.

Freddy had a moustache and a short, faded haircut. Shereece began reading his profile. He was 35 years old. His profile read: *I'm a hardworking lawyer. I love travelling and taking care of myself. I have a beautiful 6-year old daughter who means the world to me. My hobbies are playing football and table tennis. I've been single for the past two years and I am now looking for a woman to share my life with. I like a woman that knows what she wants, independent and is serious about having a long lasting relationship. If I sound like I'm the one for you, get in touch x*

'Hmmm, he's right up my street,' Shereece thought. The dating app showed if a member was on or offline, and Shereece could see that Freddy was online.

"Hi, how are you?" she messaged Freddy.

"I'm good and you?" Freddy messaged back immediately.

"I'm good. Where are you from Freddy?"

"I'm from Colchester. What about you Shereece, where are you from? And how are you finding matchup?"

"I'm from Bluendale in Essex, and I've only just joined the app, but it's alright I suppose. You're my first match."

"Ok, I know Bluendale, I have a cousin that lives there."

"Oh really? What's your cousin's name? I might know them."

"That would be telling. Lol."
"Lol," Shereece messaged back.

Chapter 14

Dating

Shereece and Freddy are out at an Italian restaurant named Frankie's in Colchester. After messaging back and forth on the dating app Shereece had signed up to, they exchanged numbers and got to talking over the phone.

Two weeks after they started talking, Freddy asked Shereece out on a date. It was a Saturday evening. Freddy and Shereece were sitting opposite each other at the dinner table.

Freddy looked as good to Shereece in person as he did on his profile pictures. Freddy had on a black suit with a black long sleeve shirt and white tie. Shereece was wearing a red high neck dress with a pair of red high heel Prada shoes on her feet. Her nail varnish on her fingers and toes was also red and her black hair was tied back in a bun.

"You look smart," Shereece said to Freddy.

"Yes, I always do," Freddy arrogantly replied. "So, have you been to an Italian restaurant before?" Freddy asked.

"Actually, no I haven't. That's why I'm excited to be here."

"I'm glad you're excited. What type of food do you usually eat?"

"I'm very versatile when it comes to food. I usually cook at home. I love lasagne and spaghetti Bolognese," Shereece said as she smiled.

"Oh, that's great, they've got both on the menu," said Freddy with the menu opened up in his hands.

"Yeah I'm not going to order any of them though. I'd like to try something I haven't tasted before," said Shereece while looking at her own menu. An Italian waitress with short black hair came to their table.

"Hi! Are you ready to place your orders?" she asked.

"No not just yet," said Freddy while still looking at his menu. Shereece thought Freddy's manners were rude due to the fact that he didn't even look at the waitress.

"Well would you both like a drink in the meantime?" asked the waitress.

"Yes, I'll get a glass of red wine," said Freddy, still looking at the menu.

"No problem. And one for you too?" the waitress asked as she looked at Shereece smiling.

"Oh, I'll just have a glass of coke," Shereece replied.

"Er, no you won't. You'll get wine just like me. I'm not drinking alone," said Freddy as he put his right hand on top of Shereece's left wrist. 'He's bossy,' Shereece thought to herself, 'How dare he put his hand on me!'

"I'm driving," said Shereece as she took her wrist back.

"So am I, but one glass isn't going to hurt," Freddy replied.

"Sigh, make that two glasses of red wine," said Shereece to the waitress.

"Ok, two glasses of red wine coming up," said the waitress with a big smile. Then she walked away.

"So Shereece, how long have you lived in Bluendale?" Freddy asked.

"I've lived there all my life. What about you? How long have you lived in Colchester?"

"I've been living in Colchester for the past five years. I'm originally from Catford in London."

"Oh really? I've heard of Catford but never been there. What made you move to Colchester then?"

"I moved to Colchester to be with my ex-girlfriend. That's where she lives. We got engaged."

"So what happened between you two then? How come it didn't work out?"

"I caught her cheating," Freddy said as he shrugged his shoulders.

"Oh wow. I'm sorry to hear that."

"Don't be. I'm glad I caught the two-timing bitch before I married her. Her loss anyway. I mean look at me. What woman in her right mind would want to cheat on a beautiful face like this?" Freddy asked while pointing at his face, smiling.

"Well, you're a confident one. aren't you?" said Shereece.

"Of course I am. You've got to be, haven't you?"

The waitress came back to the table with two large servings of red wine and placed the glasses on the table.

"Thank you," said Shereece to the waitress, while Freddy remained quiet.

"You're welcome. Are you both ready to order any food yet or do you still need more time?" asked the waitress.

"I'm ready. Can I get garlic bread for the starter, and spaghetti carbonara for my main please?" asked Shereece.

"No problem," said the waitress as she jotted the order down on her notepad, "and yourself?" said the waitress to Freddy.

"I will have the meatball Parmesan for starters, and a pasta e fagioli for my main," said Freddy.

"Good choices. I'll be with you as soon as the starters are ready," said the waitress after jotting Freddy's order down. She then walked away.

"Have you ordered that before?" asked Shereece.

"Yes, I've had it before here and it's delicious," Freddy replied while rubbing his hands together.

"It looks tasty on the menu," said Shereece.

"Oh believe me it is. I haven't had spaghetti carbonara before."

"I've never had pasta e fagiola."

"Fagioli," said Freddy correcting Shereece.

"Oh, whatever. I've never had it before," said Shereece as she laughed.

"It's a type of soup with pasta and beans."

"Yeah I read it on the menu."

"I'll tell you what, I'll try some of your main and you can try some of mine," said Freddy.

"That's fine with me," said Shereece smiling. Shereece took a sip of her wine and Freddy took a sip of his.

"So Freddy, what made you like my profile on the dating app?"

"Honestly, I liked your physique. I found your muscular figure very unique and sexy," said Freddy while looking her up and down.

"Is that it? Just my figure is what did it for you?" Shereece said, sounding a bit annoyed.

"No not just that. I also liked what I read in your profile. I liked how blunt you were. The way you didn't pussy foot around about what you want. I also found that sexy."

"Ok, I'll have you know I'm a very direct woman, and you read right, I don't pussy foot about at all."

"Good. So, tell me Shereece, as we decided not to get into too much detail over the phone. You never told me much about your family. Do you have any siblings?"

"Yes I do. I have a twin sister."

"Oh, wow! Really? That's so hot. I've never dated a twin before. So is it just you and your sister then?"

"Yes just the two of us."

"I bet you two are real close."

"What makes you say that?" asked Shereece as she took another sip of her wine.

"Well twins are always close, aren't they?" said Freddy leaning back on his chair.

"Nope not necessarily."

"Ok I'm getting the hint that you're not close to yours."

"We're close enough."

"Ok. Do you have any children?"

"Yes I do. I have two beautiful twin girls."

"No way!" Freddy exclaimed in shock. "You're a twin and you have twins. Wow. It's got to be a genetic thing that runs in your family."

"Must be," said Shereece as she smiled.

"So how old are they? Your twin girls I mean, and what's the deal with you and their father?"

"You ask a lot of questions, don't you?"

"Well how else am I going to get to know you without asking questions?" said Freddy as Shereece chuckled.

"Well, the father of my children is not around. He left when I fell pregnant. It's complicated, but yeah, he's not in the picture at all."

"Well, I'm sorry to hear that. A father should always be in their children's life. I'll never walk out on my daughter no matter what."

"That's good. So, what's your daughter's name?"

"Isobel," said Freddy as he smiled.

"Nice name."

"Thanks. I named her myself."

"Nice. So, is your ex-fiancé the mother of your daughter?"

"No she's not. My daughter came from a previous relationship before my ex. We didn't work out."

"How come? Didn't you try to make it work for your daughter's sake?"
"What happened was we got together too soon. She fell pregnant three months after we met, and by the time we got to know each we realised we were totally incompatible, and to be honest I was out of her league, so I wasn't going to put up with anything below my standards.

'How arrogant is this man,' thought Shereece.

"Where the hell is our food?!" said Freddy looking over Shereece's shoulder. "Oh here she comes," said Freddy referring to the waitress who was now walking through the packed restaurant towards their table.

"Here is your garlic bread, and here's your meatball Parmesan," the waitress said as she placed the two starters on the table.

"Thank you," said Shereece.

"I'm starving," said Freddy as he picked up his knife and fork and started to tuck in. Freddy was eating his food like he had never eaten before, stuffing his face with the meatballs fast and not taking his eyes off his plate. Shereece looked on in disgust.

"These meatballs are good. Mmmm," said Freddy as he filled up his mouth.

"I'm going to go and use the bathroom," said Shereece excusing herself from the table.

"Oh, no problem," said Freddy with his mouth full.
Shereece went into the ladies' room and stood in front of a mirror. 'He's gorgeous looking, but he's all the way up his own arse, and has terrible table manners. I am definitely not taking him seriously,' Shereece thought to herself.

Meanwhile Kia was feeding Shyla milk in the basement. Shereece had left Kia out of her coffin to care of the babies but had kept her ankles bound.

Knowing Kia was weak from the pregnancy and taking the key for the basement trap door, Shereece was confident that Kia couldn't escape if she tried. But Kia had plans of escaping.

After feeding Shyla and Peree, she got on her knees and started crawling around the huge basement, looking for any type of weapon she could find. She couldn't seem to find anything until she came across a medium sized cream coloured wooden box on the far right hand side of the basement placed right up against the wall behind Shereece's bench press.

The box was 20 cm in height and 28 cm in width. There was a lock on the box that Kia could see, but she attempted to open the box lid anyway. To her surprise the box was unlocked. Kia was shocked at what she saw inside.

The box was filled with weapons, ranging from a hand gun to knives and handcuffs. Kia took out a Rambo shaped knife that had a knuckle duster handle. She put her fingers through the handle and made a stabbing motion.

Kia had never done anything violent before, but she was keen to get out of her hostage situation, and if killing Shereece was her way of saving herself and her babies, then she was willing to do it. Kia put down the Rambo knife and picked up the handgun.

She had never held a gun before. It was a black beretta. 'This is probably the same gun Shereece used to kill Derrick with,' Kia thought to herself. Tears started to roll down Kia's cheeks as she thought about Derrick and how Shereece killed him. "I'm so sorry Derrick," Kia said to herself.

Then Kia's emotions turned into rage. "I'm going to avenge you baby, I promise. AHHHHHH!" Kia screamed to the top of her voice and fired the gun in her hand pointed towards the basement wall in front of her. The gun clicked but there was no loud sound. Kia used her knowledge from what she had seen in movies and cocked the gun back.

She looked into the gun chamber and could see there were no bullets. She started to ransack the box quickly to see if she could find any bullets, but there were none in the box. Kia let out a long sigh before putting the gun back in the box and picking up the Rambo knife. "This will have to do," Kia whispered to herself.

Freddy and Shereece had just finished both of their meals in Frankie's restaurant. Freddy had been going on about how good he was at his job and how well he got paid.

"I must say to you Shereece, any woman that gets with me is a lucky woman."

"Oh really?" replied Shereece.

"Fuck yeah, I'm telling you, I'm that guy. I can prove it to you."

"And how are you going to prove it to me?" Freddy looked into Shereece's eyes. "Come home with me tonight and all will be proven," said Freddy placing his hand on top of Shereece's right hand.

"I don't think so," said Shereece as she pulled her hand away. Shereece was strongly attracted to Freddy's appearance but could sense he was just after a quick fuck.

"Don't be like that baby. What's the problem? You do fancy me, don't you?" asked Freddy.

"I think we should get the bill now," said Shereece as she waved over the waitress who had served them earlier. The waitress came to the table.

"Can we get the bill please?" asked Shereece.

"No problem. I'll be back in two ticks," replied the waitress.

"Should I take that as a no?" said Freddy.

"Take what as a no?"

"I asked you if you fancied me."

"You're an attractive guy, but it's too early to say if I like you. It's only our first date. Let's see how things go."

"So you will see me again then?" Freddy asked keenly. 'He so full on,' Shereece thought to herself.

"We'll see," Shereece replied, not wanting to commit.

"We'll see?" Freddy repeated with a big smile on his face before bursting out with laughter. "Hahahaha" Freddy laughed.

The waitress came back to their table and laid down the bill. Freddy picked up the bill.

"£75.99. Are we going to go halves?" Freddy asked Shereece with a big grin on his face.

"Excuse me? You're not even going to pay the bill? Don't worry about it I'll pay my half then I'm gone!" said Shereece annoyed as she delved into her purse.

"I'm just kidding," said Freddy as he reached over and held Shereece's arm to stop her rustling through her purse. "You really think I'll make you pay? I've got this don't worry. You don't pay for anything when you're out with me," said Freddy confidently.

Freddy put his hand into the inside of his black blazer pocket and took out his wallet. He pulled out two £50 notes and placed them on the bill plate.

"Keep the change," said Freddy to the waitress.

"Oh! Thank you so much," said the waitress smiling.

"Forgive him, I could see he was just joking," said the waitress to Shereece, referring to Freddy asking to go halves on the bill.

"You know you both look cute together. You really suit," said the waitress to them both.

"Thank you," said Shereece.

"Have a great night," said the waitress before picking up the bill and walking away. "She was nice, wasn't she?" said Shereece.

"She was alright," said Freddy.

"Well, she must have been better than alright for you to give her a £24 tip."

"That's nothing, I always leave tips. I have the money," said Freddy arrogantly. Shereece had to resist from rolling her eyes.

"You talk about your money so much, and you were going to have me pay half," said Shereece.

"I told you I was only kidding."

"Hmmm, if you say so. Well, are you ready?"

"Ready when you are."

"Ok then, let's go. I've got to be getting back home."

Shereece and Freddy both got up and headed out of the restaurant.

"Let me walk you to your car," said Freddy to Shereece after leaving the restaurant.

"It's fine, I'll be ok."

"Come on. Let me be a gentleman and walk you to your car."

Shereece sighed, "Ok if you insist." Freddy grabbed hold of Shereece's left hand and they began walking.

"So, what would you be doing right now if you weren't here with me Shereece?" Freddy asked.

"I'd be looking after my babies."

"Who's looking after them now?"

"A friend. One of my best friends. She said she'll have them for me tonight seeing as I don't go out much. She's such a bestie. I love her to bits," Shereece lied.

"That's nice to have friends like that. You're lucky."

"I am. So where's your daughter tonight? I assume she's at her mother's."

"Actually, she's at my mother's. She stays at my mother's every other weekend. She loves her grandmother."

"That's nice."

"Where are your parents from Shereece?"

"My father is Scottish and my mother was from Ghana."

"Was?"

"Yeah, she passed away at childbirth."

"Sorry to hear that," Freddy said sympathetically.

"It's ok." Shareece said as they arrived at her car.

"So, this is where we say goodbye," said Freddy. Freddy then put both his arms around Shereece's waist and leaned in for a kiss. Shereece closed her eyes and allowed Freddy to kiss her. Freddy slipped his tongue in Shereece's mouth and they kissed deeply. Freddy lowered the palm of his right hand down to Shereece's buttocks. Shereece pulled away and smacked Freddy's hand.

"We're in public, don't be naughty," said Shereece blushing with embarrassment.

"Come back to mine with me," said Freddy.

"No way. It's our first date, behave."

"Forget all that first date nonsense. If we're feeling for each other, that's all that matters."

"I can't. Not tonight. I've got to get home to my babies. Besides it's too soon."

"Come on, just for a little while. I'll make it worth your while," said Freddy putting one arm around Shereece's waist.

"And how will you make it worth my while?" asked Shereece with her chin up. Freddy leaned in to Shereece and started to kiss her neck. Shereece closed her eyes enjoying the feeling.

Freddy slowly went from kissing, to sucking on Shereece's neck.

"Ooh that feels so good," said Shereece with her eyes still closed. 'Maybe I should just go with him and fuck his brains out. Yeah he is arrogant, but he looks sexy as fuck,' Shereece thought.

"Ok let's do it, let's just do it." Shereece said in excitement as she pulled away from Freddy.

Freddy looked at Shereece with a big grin, happy that she came around.

"Where are you parked?" Shereece asked.

"Just two cars behind yours." Freddy took out his car key and pointed it towards his red Porsche, then pressed the unlock button. Shereece looked behind her and saw the car lights flash.

"That's your car?" asked Shereece impressed.

"Well, I wouldn't have the keys if it wasn't," said Freddy sarcastically. Shereece bowed her head and looked at Freddy with a devilish smile.

"You have a nice car," said Shereece.

"I know I do. I'm going to pull up in front of you, then you just follow me ok," said Freddy.

By now Shereece was already in the driver's seat with her engine on. She pulled out of the parking space and began to follow Freddy as he pulled away.

It was a fifteen-minute drive to Freddy's house. Freddy pulled up onto his driveway while Shereece pulled into a space opposite Freddy's house. She then looked at the quiet street she was parked in and observed the posh looking houses. 'What a nice street,' she thought.

Freddy got out of his Porsche and walked to the left hand side of Shereece's car. Shereece rolled her window down.

Freddy popped his head into her car and said, "Well here we are babes."

"So this is where you live?"

"Yeah. Come on let me show you inside, it's cold out here."

"Will I be ok parking here? I don't want to get a ticket."

"You'll be fine right here. This whole road is free parking. Come on let's go."

"Ok." Freddy popped his head out of her car. Shereece turned the ignition off then got out of the car. She walked round to the passenger side of her car where Freddy was standing.

Freddy took hold of Shereece's hand and walked her to the front door of his house. He then went into his trouser pocket and brought out his key ring finding his house key to open the front door. He led Shereece into his house and switched on the corridor lights.

Freddy's corridor was long, and it led to an open space living room and kitchen. His floors were laminated and were light grey. His walls were bright white with several framed pictures of himself and of his daughter.

"Come in. Let me show you around my pad," said Freddy proudly as he walked Shereece through to his open plan living room and he turned on the living room light. The room instantly brightened. It was spacious and clean. The ceiling lights were made from crystal. Freddy had a long, black leather sofa that was opposite his 72inch plasma TV. In between the TV and the sofa was a beautiful round glass table. More pictures of Freddy were framed on the right hand side of his living room wall.

"This is a nice place you have here Freddy."

"I know," Freddy replied smiling.

"You're good at saying 'I know', aren't you?" said Shereece as she looked at Freddy. Freddy laughed.

"Sit down. Let me pour a drink," said Freddy.

"No, I like to be sober when I fuck," replied Shereece. There were a few seconds of silence between Freddy and Shereece as they stared at each other after Shereece's blunt comment. Then they both pounced on each other. They started kissing and dragging off each other's clothes aggressively.

Freddy unzipped the back of Shereece's dress, then pulled it down. Shereece then put her hands behind her back and unhooked her bra, revealing her B cup size breasts. She then shoved Freddy's head onto her right breast and Freddy began to suck on her nipple.

"Ooooh," Shereece groaned in pleasure. Freddy tried to pull his head up but Shereece still had a tight grip on the back of his head and wouldn't let loose.

"Suck it," Shereece said. Freddy continued sucking. "Oooh ahhh," Shereece continued to moan.

Freddy again tried to release his head from Shereece's grip but Shereece wouldn't let loose.

"Suck it more!" she said loudly. Freddy shoved Shereece's hand off the back of his head and stood up letting out a brief laugh.

"You like to be in control, don't you? Well tonight I'm in control," said Freddy.

"You don't know me," said Shereece as she shook her head. Freddy took a step back from Shereece and stared her up and down, looking at her now half naked body.

"Come with me," Freddy said as he took Shereece by her left wrist. He took her back through his corridor then up a long flight of stairs that led to the second floor of his house. When they got to the top of the stairs, Freddy took Shereece into his bedroom that was so dark Shereece couldn't see.

"Aren't you going to turn on the light?" asked Shereece. Freddy went beside his double sized black leather bed and switched on a yellow lamp that was standing on his black bedside cabinet.

Freddy then sat on his bed and began taking off the remainder of his clothes. First his long sleeve shirt, then his vest, revealing a chiselled, dark skinned chest and stomach.

Then he removed his shoes and trousers, leaving him in only his boxers and socks. Shereece looked at Freddy's body lustfully.

Freddy put up his right hand and used his index finger to beckon Shereece over. Shereece walked over to Freddy until her belly button was right next to his nose. Freddy pulled down Shereece's red French knickers, then pulled her on top of him.

As they began kissing, Freddy squeezed on both of Shereece's firm butt cheeks. Shereece started to suck on the right side of Freddy's neck.

"Ohhhhh, I like that," said Freddy. He then slipped his middle finger into Shereece's now moist vagina.

"Aaaah," Shereece moaned. He started twirling his finger in Shereece's vagina. Shereece moaned louder.

"Enough of this," said Freddy before rolling Shereece to his right and getting on top of her. He quickly took off his boxers, spread her legs with his and attempted to push his erect penis inside of her. Shereece blocked Freddy's dick with her right hand.

"Put something on or you're not going in."

"Ok.... ok," Freddy said with a smile. He then went into the first drawer of his bedside cabinet and took out a red Durex condom.

"Here you go baby," he said as he waved the condom in the air. He then tore open the condom packet with his teeth, took the condom out and rolled it down his erection. Freddy then got back on top of Shereece and attempted to enter her again before Shereece blocked his penis with her inner thighs.

"What's wrong? I've got the condom on," said Freddy in confusion.

"Go down on me first," said Shereece.

"What? Nah, I don't do that," said Freddy as he shook his head.

"Go on, just do it. Eat my clit."

"I'm not doing that! Just come on, let me fuck you," said Freddy as he tried to force himself into Shereece. Shereece squeezed hard on Freddy's erect penis with her right hand.

"Arrrrrh! What the fuck are you doing?!" screamed Freddy.

"If you don't lick my pussy we're not fucking," said Shereece bluntly as she sat up.

"You know what? You're hard work!" said Freddy loudly and breathing heavily in frustration, whilst holding his penis.

"No problem, I'll just leave," said Shereece as she got up.

"No don't," said Freddy as he held both of Shereece's arms by the biceps. "I'll do it."

Freddy slowly pulled Shereece back down on his bed. He then got on his knees and spread her legs apart. Freddy was now directly facing Shereece's shaved vagina. He lowered his head and started sucking Shereece's clit.

"Ahhhh, yes," Shereece moaned as she rubbed the back of Freddy's head. "Harder, suck it harder.

Freddy sucked and licked Shereece's clitoris as hard as he could. The moans of joy from Shereece were arousing Freddy.

"Keep going, I'm cumming, I'm cumming!" Shereece moaned loudly. Freddy proceeded to suck her clitoris until finally Shereece orgasmed.

"Oh, wow!" Shereece said as she took deep breaths. Freddy looked up at Shereece's face and smiled as she looked down at him. He crawled up on to Shereece's body until they were head to head and tried to put his still erect penis inside of her vagina. Shereece swiftly pushed Freddy off her and got up, leaving Freddy on his side lying on the bed.

"What.... what's the problem?" asked Freddy confused with his arms out.

"There's no problem, I've just got to go."

"Ballshit bitch! You're not going nowhere," said Freddy loudly as he got up angry, and aggressively grabbed Shereece's left arm. "You're going to lie down and I'm going to fuck you."

"You better get off my arm or you're gonna regret it," Shereece warned Freddy looking him straight in his dark brown eyes.

"Fuck you," said Freddy bluntly. Then he dragged Shereece down on the bed and got on top of her. "This pussy is mine. You want to play hard to get? Cool, but this pussy is mine."

"I'm not playing hard to get, prick," said Shereece. Then she grabbed Freddy's neck in a chokehold. She squeezed on Freddy's neck so hard that Freddy started to cough. Freddy desperately tried to loosen Shereece's grip on his neck with his hands, but Shereece's grip was too strong.

"I bet you regret not letting me leave now, don't you? You fucking prick! What do you think I pump weights for huh?.....huhhh?!"

Shereece manoeuvred on top of Freddy while still squeezing on his neck.

"Ple..plea...please let me...let me go," Freddy stuttered. Shereece's face was screwed up. Her killer instinct made her want to kill Freddy, but she started to think logically about the situation and realised it would be too easy for her to get caught having not planned the kill. She loosened her grip on Freddy's neck and let him go. Once released, Freddy started coughing uncontrollably.

"I'm out of here dick," said Shereece before heading downstairs. She put all her clothes back on, then headed out the house. Freddy came running downstairs to the front door half naked.

"You fucking bitch! You're not going to a get away with this, trust me!" Freddy shouted out in his doorway.

Shereece looked back at Freddy and laughed at him. She then got into her car, put her home address in her satnav, switched on the ignition and began her drive home.

Thirty minutes later Shereece pulled up on her driveway, and exited her car. She walked to her front door and opened it, then headed for the basement.

Walking down the basement steps, Shereece could see Shyla and Peree sleeping in their cot. When she got to the bottom of the steps, she looked at Kia's open coffin and could see Kia wasn't in it

"Kia! Kia where are you!" Shereece called. "Aaaaah!" Shereece screamed out feeling a burst of pain in her right calf muscle. Kia had stabbed her in the leg with the Rambo knife.

Shereece turned around to see Kia on her knees holding the bloodied knife. "You fucking bitch!" Shereece shouted. Kia then fully emerged from behind the steps where she was hiding and plunged the knife at Shereece again but missed as Shereece moved her leg out the way and booted Kia in the face. Kia fell back and dropped the knife on the floor.

Shereece went for the knife but so did Kia. Kia beat her to the chase. Kia spat blood out her mouth and fought back as Shereece attempted to take the knife from her. She aimed the knife in Shereece's direction, swinging it left to right. Kia used the handrail of the staircase to pull herself up onto her feet.

Holding onto the staircase with one arm and pointing the knife at Shereece with the other. Kia and Shereece were having a stand-off.

"COME ON! COME ON!" Kia screamed. Both the babies woke up crying.

"You've woken up the babies!" Shereece said out loud in anger.

"Fuck you! If you really cared about the babies you'd let us go. Now get me the fuck out of here!" Shereece smiled at Kia deviously.

"I admire your courage Kia, but see, there's no point in trying to fight me. You're too weak, besides if I wanted to, I could just get my gun and blow your head off. It's that simple. But I don't want to do that Kia. I just want us to be one happy family."

"Is that so? What's that? Is that perfume I smell on you, ha? What, you've been out on a date? There's no way you can let someone find out about me. It's only a matter of time before you kill me; just like you killed Derrick, you fucking murderer!" Kia shouted out.

"I don't want to kill you Kia. I want you to join me and my religion."

"I don't want to join you and your fucking religion. I want to get out of here with my babies. Now unshackle me, now!"

"You know I can't do that Kia. You're breaking all my rules."

"Fuck you and your fucking rules and get me the fuck out of here!"

Shereece tutted and started limping to the right hand side of the basement where she kept her wooden weapons box. Her right leg was bleeding heavily, but Shereece ignored the mess and pain. She got to the box and took out her beretta handgun. Shereece then walked back towards Kia and stopped when they were a few feet apart from each other, then aimed the gun at Kia's chest. Kia clenched the Rambo knife firmly in her hand and pulled her arm back ready to lunge at Shereece with it.

"Put the knife down Kia or I'll put a bullet through your fucking chest," Shereece said in a deadly calm voice.

"Go on then bitch. Shoot! SHOOT!" Kia shouted in anger, taunting her sister. "I know you haven't got any more bullets. As you know I've already been in your box. Wasn't very smart to leave it unlocked was it?!"

Shereece started breathing heavily with anger. "Arrrrrgh!" Shereece screamed at the top of her voice and charged into Kia.

Kia swung the knife at Shereece but Shereece caught Kia by the wrist blocking the attack. Shereece then pistol-whipped Kia three times on the side of her head. Kia passed out and fell to the ground. Shereece bent down and whispered in Kia's ear "Just off the record bitch I do have more bullets." She then left the basement with the babies still crying, the gun in her hand and went into her back garden. She lifted up a cement slab that was beside the lawn. Under the slab was a blue bag full of sixteen hollow point bullets. Shereece put ten of them in her gun clip, slapped the clip in the gun and put the remaining six back under the cement slab.

Chapter 15

Shereece's Slaves

"Yes mum. I heard you the first time, I'll do the dishes when I get back!" Ricky shouted at his mother before slamming the house front door behind him.

Ricky still lived with his mother in Bluendale. He had no job but received money through disability benefits. He was legally considered to have severe mental health problems and therefore unfit to work. Most of his disability benefits went on Shereece. Every month she would demand he pay her a large portion of his benefits, and he would gladly do so. He had no children or partner. His only devotion in life was to please his Mistress Lilith.

Ricky got into his car that was parked outside his mother's house. He turned the ignition on and began driving. While driving, his old Samsung mobile phone began ringing. Ricky hastily took the phone out of his left trouser, looked at the phone screen and saw Mistress Lilith's incoming call. He pressed the answer button on the phone then put the phone to his ear.

"Where are you?" asked Mistress Lilith on the other end of the line.

"I'm on my way Mistress."

"Hurry up, you're running late. You know this is unacceptable," said Shereece sharply.

"I'm sorry Mistress. I just had a bit of house issues. I won't be long."

"Don't tell me about your house issues, just hurry up and get your arse here!"

"Yes Mistress."

Shereece then cut off the phone.

Ricky put his foot down hard on the accelerator, desperate to get to Shereece's house as quickly as possible. When he finally arrived, he parked opposite her house, got out of his car and walked to Shereece's front door before ringing her doorbell.

A minute went by before Shereece opened the door and said, "What time do you call this?"

"I'm sorry Mistress Lilith. I promise it won't happen again."

"You're going to be punished for your poor punctuality. Now get inside." Ricky walked in. Shereece closed the front door behind him then led the way to the basement. As they got to the bottom of the basement stairs, Ricky noticed the babies and the cot were gone.

"Where are your babies Mistress?"

"They're in my room now. They will no longer be staying down here."

Ricky followed Shereece into the middle of the basement where he saw Victor naked on his knees with his hands together and eyes closed.

In front of Victor was a circle of candles, and in the middle of the circle was the shape of a pentagram drawn on the basement floor with chalk.

"Get naked, then get on your knees and worship our lord Satan," said Shereece.

Ricky did what he was told. Once fully naked, he got on to his knees opposite Victor and began to repeat the words, "Hail Satan!" Shereece got on her knees on the right hand side of the candles and repeated the words, "Hail Satan! This week Ricky, you'll be put on an assignment. We're going to make another sacrifice to Satan, but this time it must be someone you love, someone very close to you. To prove your devotion to me and your lord Satan, it must be the blood of one of your loved ones. Will you handle this Ricky?"

Ricky went quiet for a few seconds before saying, "But what about Victor? How come he doesn't have to sacrifice someone he loves?"

"Who said he doesn't?!" Shereece snapped. "One at a time. Victor will make his sacrifice after you make yours. Is there a problem Ricky? Because if there is then you don't belong in this circle anymore," Shereece told him bluntly. Ricky rubbed his head and let out a light sigh.

Out of fear of being kicked out of her circle, he replied, "No Mistress Lilith, there's no problem at all."

"Good. So, who will it be Ricky?"

"Well I'm not sure right now."

"It will be your mother. I know she is close to you. You will sacrifice her for your cult, and if you don't do it you're out. But if you do then you get to eat my pussy."

"Ok Mistress Lilith. Ok, I'll do it," said Ricky firmly.

"You'll have to bring her here. All sacrifices must be made in this basement," said Shereece.

"I'm not sure how I'm going to get her here Mistress. Mother doesn't like leaving the house anymore. She barely leaves the house for anything these days. I go out and do the shopping for her. She only goes outside to do gardening and that's it."

"You'll have to drug her. Drug her to sleep then drive her here. I have just the right drugs you will need to spike her with," said Shereece.

Ricky's mind was now racing. He started to think about all the nagging and insults his mum would throw at him. Calling him useless and telling him to get off his arse and find a job.

"You're just like your father was. Good for nothing!" she would curse. Deep down Ricky loved his mother, but he also harboured bitterness towards her.

He feared losing favour from Mistress Lilith more than anything and was prepared to sacrifice his mother's life to prevent that from happening.

Shereece walked behind Victor and started to seduce him. She knelt behind him and put both her arms around his shoulders, then slowly started scratching his chest. She then began playing with his right earlobe with her tongue, flicking it and slowly nibbling on it. All the while she was looking in Ricky's eyes.

"How bad do you want me Ricky?" Shereece whispered seductively. Ricky was so aroused he started to shiver.

"I want you so bad Mistress Lilith."

"Crawl to me," said Shereece. Ricky already on his knees, put both his hands in front of him and crawled to Shereece. Shereece grabbed hold of Ricky's jaw and ordered him to open his mouth. Ricky obeyed. She then spat in Ricky's open mouth.

"Now swallow it like you love me," demanded Shereece. Ricky swallowed Shereece's spit. "Good boy," said Shereece as she tapped Ricky's right cheek a few times with her hand. "Now what do you say?" asked Shereece.

"Thank you Mistress Lilith," replied Ricky.

"What would you do for me?" asked Shereece.

"Anything," answered Ricky. Shereece smiled then got up onto her feet. She went to the end of the basement and came back to Ricky and Victor with two satanic bibles. She dropped them both on the floor.

"Study," she instructed before leaving them to go to Kia's coffin. Shereece knelt down and opened Kia's coffin lid. She could see Kia was awake. She leaned in to Kia to kiss her on the mouth, but Kia turned her face.

"Where are my babies?" Kia asked angrily. Shereece smiled.

"Our babies are safe and sound," replied Shereece as she stroked Kia's face. "You know you've lost your privileges of coming out of your coffin. I can't trust you anymore. What am I going to do with you Kia? I could easily kill you, but deep down I don't want to do that. I guess I love you."

"If you loved me, you'd let me go. You're never going to let me go, are you Shereece? You can't. You'll be too afraid I'll give you up to the police. Oh my God I'm going to die here," said Kia before bursting into tears. Shereece stared at Kia as she cried for a few seconds, then reached for the coffin lid to close it.

"I'm going to go check on the babies," Shereece told Kia.

"Wait a minute!" shouted Kia before Shereece could close the coffin lid. "I'll join your religion. I want to become part of it."

"You're just saying that for me to let you go. But you were right. I can't let you go. I can't trust you."

"Yes you can trust me, you can! Let me practice your religion with you. In time you'll see you can trust me."

Shereece knew that Kia could just be saying what she thought she wanted to hear, but still Shereece couldn't deny the good feeling she felt at the thought that her sister could be part of her cult and partner in crime. Shereece wanted someone more intelligent than her slaves to be her accomplice, and who better than her twin sister.

"If you are going to join my cult, you will have to kill. We make human sacrifices," said Shereece.

"Fine, I'll do so."

"We'll see" said Shereece before closing the coffin lid. She got up and walked up her basement stairs with a big smile on her face.

"Hush little baby don't say a word, mamma's gonna buy you a mockingbird, and if that mocking bird don't sing, mamma's gonna buy you a diamond ring, and if that diamond ring is brass, mamma's gonna buy you a looking glass," Shereece sung away to Shyla and Peree as she held them both in her arms after feeding them. She was now in her bedroom where she had moved the babies to, sitting on her bed, rocking back and forth with the babies in her arms.

Two weeks had passed by since Shereece had ordered Ricky to sacrifice his mother. It was a Saturday night when Shereece called him: "Have you done it yet!" Shereece said at the other end of Ricky's phone.

"No Mistress, but I will."

"What's the hold up?" she demanded to know.

"I haven't got around to making her a drink yet. She refused my last offer."

"Well try harder. This is a big night for you Ricky. Me and Victor are waiting." Shereece then hung up the phone.

Ricky went into his kitchen and began to make a cup of tea for his mother. After making the tea, he slipped in Rohypnol, the same drug Shereece had used on Derrick.

Ricky walked from the kitchen to the living room with the cup of tea.

"Here mum," said Ricky as he passed his mother the cup while she was sitting on her brown woollen couch watching TV.

Ricky's mother was in her late sixties. She wore glasses, was slim and had curly grey hair. Her face was wrinkled. She flicked her cigarette in the ash tray that was on the table in front of her, then took the cup of tea from Ricky.

"Thanks for that Ricky boy. I can actually do with a cuppa right now."

"That's alright mum." She then took a slurp of the tea.

"Ooooh! it's so hot!"

"That's because I just made it for you mum," Ricky replied with a big smile on his face as he sat down beside her.

"What's got into you today Ricky? You've washed your own dishes, you've helped tidy up the house, and you've made me a cuppa. What's up? You bumped your head or something?"

"No not at all mum. I just realised I've got to start helping you out more. I mean you're not getting any younger you know."

"No I'm not. I'm glad you've realised that. So does this mean you'll be washing your own clothes from now on then? I've had enough of having to smell those stinky socks of yours." Ricky laughed.

"Don't worry mum. You'll be seeing a brand new me from now on." Ricky's mum looked at him and said, "You really have bumped your head today."

Thirty minutes went by. Ricky's mother had finished the tea and was now conked out cold. Ricky stared at his mum who was now slouched on the couch.

He manoeuvred her body until she was lying on her back. He then took out his mobile phone and called Mistress Lilith.

"Hello," said Shereece on the other end of Ricky's line when she answered his call. "I've done it! I've done it! I've spiked her!" said Ricky in excitement.

"Is she passed out yet?"

"Yes she's out."

"Ok, put her in your car very discreetly. I mean it! Don't let anybody see you bringing her out to your car."

"Yes Mistress Lilith."

"You're doing well Ricky. Don't mess this up."

"Okay Mistress, I won't." Shereece ended the call.

Ricky turned off the TV, then picked up his mother and put her over his right shoulder. He then walked to the front door of the house and opened it slightly, enough for him to check if anybody was walking or driving past.

When Ricky could see the coast was clear, he left the house and headed straight for his car. He opened up the left side back door of the car and laid his mother down on the back seat. Ricky let out a deep sigh before walking round to the driver's side of the car and letting himself in. He started up the engine and began driving to his destination.

After the fifteen minute journey, Ricky arrived at Shereece's house. He parked outside her house and called Mistress Lilith's phone.

"Where are you?" asked Shereece when she answered the call.

"I'm parked outside Mistress." Shereece peered out of her kitchen window to see if she could see Ricky's car. She spotted it.

"Is she with you?"

"Yes Mistress, she's here with me on the backseat."

"Alright. Here is what I want you to do. Drive to the back of my house. You're going to have to bring her in through my back garden. It's too risky to bring her in through my front door. Follow the road all the way round to the left and it will lead you to the back of my house. I'll be waiting outside the garden for you." Ricky obeyed Shereece and found Shereece standing outside her back garden and parked up next to her. He opened the passenger seat window and Shereece popped her head into the car to see Ricky's mother lying motionless in the back seat. She then looked at Ricky and said, "Well done Ricky, well done. So, are you ready to make your Mistress proud tonight?"

"Yes Mistress, I am."

"Good. Bring her in."

Ricky got out of his car and opened up the car's right hand side back door. He grabbed both of his mother's arms and pulled her out the car. He then quickly put her over his right shoulder and entered Shereece's garden where she was holding the gate open for him. She closed the gate behind Ricky then walked in front of him to lead the way.

Shereece's back garden led to her living room, and once they were all in Shereece's living room, Shereece opened the trap door to the basement and waved Ricky to go down.

Ricky descended the stairs whilst holding his mother. Shereece followed behind them after closing the trap door. When they arrived at the bottom of the stairs, they both walked into the centre of the basement where there was a circle of lit candles that brightened up the basement.

Victor was surrounded by the candles and on his knees naked, wearing only a black leather mask. The mask fully covered his head and face, there were two holes so he could see out of the mask and on the mouth section there was a silver zip which was closed.

"Where should I put her?" Ricky asked Shereece.

"Right here," said Shereece as she got on her knees and started to draw a large pentagram symbol on the basement floor with chalk. Ricky put his mother on top of the symbol when Shereece finished drawing it. Shereece went into the handbag she was carrying and took out her Rambo knife. She handed the knife to Ricky.

"This is it Ricky. Moment of truth. Kill her," said Shereece to Ricky who was now holding the Rambo knife in his clenched fist.

Ricky stood over his mother's body.

"Ricky...Ricky, where....where am I?" Ricky's mother stuttered as she was starting to come out of her drugged daze. Her vision was blurry. She was seeing double of Ricky's body as she looked up.

"Do it, do it!" said Shereece. Victor unzipped the mouth piece on his mask and began to chant, "Do it, do it!" along with Shereece.

Shereece and Victor were now both chanting out loud, "DO IT! DO IT! DO IT!" with their fists pumping up and down in the air as they said it. Ricky hesitated. He began having flash backs in his mind about times when his mother had made him breakfast before going to school, and even more times of her washing and ironing his clothes for him.

But then he started to think about all the moaning, nagging, screaming and shouting he endured from her about him not cleaning up after himself, not being able to move out of her house and getting himself a job.

The chanting then started to excite Ricky.

"DO IT! DO IT! DO IT!" Victor and Shereece chanted. Ricky took a look at Victor chanting, then looked at Shereece chanting, then he looked at his mother lying on the floor.

"You're history mum!" shouted Ricky before sitting on his mother's chest and slicing her throat from ear to ear. Blood gushed out of her neck and splattered across Ricky's face. She started coughing out large amounts of blood. Her eyes widened so large it looked like they were going to come out of her sockets.

"Yes! yes! die! die!" Shereece screamed as she watched Ricky's mother shake and choke. Ricky got up and stood over his mother's body.

"Die! die!" shouted Victor, happily going along with Shereece's chants.

Seconds passed by before Ricky's mother stopped moving. Her eyes rolled to the back of her head as she died.

Shereece got on her knees and rubbed her hands on Ricky's mother's slashed throat. With her hands now covered in blood, Shereece slipped her fingers into her vagina and began pleasuring herself while shouting "Hail Satan! Hail Satan!"

Ricky and Victor both began chanting, "Hail Satan!" loudly with Shereece. "Uhh! uhh! uhh!" Shereece started to moan loudly as she rapidly played with her clitoris.

"Uhh! uhh!" Shereece let out two more moans and then a big sigh as she climaxed over her bloody fingers. She then got up and rubbed her hands over Ricky's forehead before putting two of her fingers in his mouth. Ricky sucked Shereece's fingers. Then she went to Victor and put her bloodied fingers in his mouth. Victor also sucked the blood off of her fingers.

"Hail Satan," Shereece said while looking down at Victor. She then turned around and looked at Ricky. "Get on your knees Ricky." Ricky did as he was told. Shereece then walked over to him and held his head with both her hands while standing in front of him. She loosened her dressing gown. Her blood smeared vagina was now fully exposed to Ricky's face.

"I keep my word. Eat me."

"Yes Mistress." Ricky then began to suck and lick Shereece's vagina. After pleasuring herself by rubbing her clit on Ricky's face and mouth, Shereece took her knife away from Ricky then sat on his mother's stomach. She then plunged the knife as hard as she could into his mother's chest and sliced it open.

"This ritual isn't complete until we taste the blood of her heart," said Shereece.

She then ferociously stuffed her right hand into the big gash that was now in Ricky's mother's chest and dragged her heart out. She stabbed the heart that was in her hand, then she held the heart over her head. Blood spurted out of the heart and over Shereece's head and face.

Shereece held her tongue out and collected some of the blood into her mouth. She got up on to her feet and held the heart over Ricky's head.

"Open your mouth," she said to Ricky. Ricky opened his mouth and collected the blood that was dripping down his face with his tongue. She then squeezed the heart over Victor's head. Victor also held out his tongue and drank blood from the heart.

"Hail Satan! Hail Satan!" Shereece chanted. Victor and Ricky chanted along with her.

After the ritual, Shereece cleaned up all the blood, washed and dried Ricky and Victor's clothes, and put Ricky's mother's corpse into one of her empty coffins.

After they all got clean in her shower, she sent Ricky and Victor home before going to bed in her room and sleeping soundly.

The very next morning, Shereece woke up to Shyla and Peree crying. She got out of her bed and leaned over the babies' cot.

"Ahh how's my little munchkins. Mummy is going to make you some milk ok. I'll be right back," said Shereece.

She went into her kitchen and quickly made them their milk. She came back into the bedroom where the babies were still crying. She put the milk bottles on a desk that was beside her bed before taking the babies out of the cot.

Once both the babies were in her arms, she picked up the bottles and simultaneously fed them.

"We're going to get some fresh air today my little pumpkins. Just the three of us. We're going to go shopping, then for a nice stroll in the park," said Shereece.

She now wanted to show off the twins to the world. Once Shereece finished feeding the babies, she started to get ready for the day. She showered, moisturised, then put on her grey adidas tracksuit. After getting fully dressed, she changed the babies and dressed them. She then brought them downstairs and placed them on the living room sofa. She went under the staircase and took out the double pram she had bought. She strapped both babies into the pram before heading down to the basement. She opened Kia's coffin to check in on her. Kia struggled to open her eyes.

"I'm going out with the babies. Is there anything you want me to get you from the outside?"

"When will you be back?" Kia asked.

"Around noonish."

"I'm kind of hungry right now. Could you fix me a breakfast before you leave please?"

Shereece stared into Kia's eyes for a moment before saying, "Sure. We've got sausages, eggs and hash browns," said Shereece.

"That will be great," replied Kia gratefully.

Shereece cooked Kia her breakfast and then fed it to her.

"Right, I've got to go now," said Shereece getting up and reaching for the coffin lid.

"Wait.... I heard what you were doing last night. Your ritual, Hail Satan. Is that how you praise him?" asked Kia.

"There's much more to it than that."

"Show me the much more."

"I can't. The last time I let you out, it almost cost me my leg, remember?" said Shereece as she showed Kia the stitched-up wound.

"Please Shereece, I'm being genuine. Nothing like that will happen again. I need something to do. I'd like something to do. I've been in here over a year now. I've accepted I'm your property. I just want to be a part of your lifestyle now. Please let me." Kia's pleas sounded sincere.

"As I've already told you, to be part of what I'm into you will have to kill."

"That's ok with me. I'm willing to do that."

"To gain your freedom?"

"To gain your love Shereece." Kia moved her cuffed hands up to her left breast and pulled her blouse over it, exposing her breast for Shereece to see. "I know you want me Shereece." Shereece looked at Kia's bare breast with lust.

"I've got to go shopping with the babies," Shereece whispered.

"Come here Shereece." Shereece bent down to Kia. "Kiss me," said Kia softly. Shereece leaned down to Kia's face. They locked lips and kissed for a few seconds. Shereece stroked Kia's face.

"I've got to go now," said Shereece before grabbing on to the coffin lid.

"You've finally come around then?" said Shereece looking down at Kia.

"Yes," replied Kia confidently.

"We'll see." Shereece closed the coffin lid, locked it then exited the basement with a smile on her face. She was happy that Kia wanted to be with her sexually, and she was happy she wanted to join her cult. Shereece believed that Kia was sincere about what she was saying, mainly because she so badly wanted it to be true.

Shereece took the babies out the house in the pram and decided to walk instead of drive to the local food centre that was a ten-minute walk up the road from her.

While walking she bumped into one of her old nursery colleagues named Karen, a young five-foot four, petite, white lady with short brown hair which showed off her slim pretty face.

"Hi Shereece how are you? Long time," said Karen smiling.

"I'm fine honey, how are you?"

"I'm good." They shared a brief hug. "And who are these lovely munchkins here," said Karen as she bent down to look at the babies."

"They're my little twins. Say hello to Shyla and Peree." Karen gasped and put her hand on her chest.

"No way, these are yours?" Karen stood up and held Shereece's left arm. "Shereece I'm so shocked. Oh my God. You know there was a rumour going around that you couldn't actually have-"

"No that's not true," Shereece interrupted. "I had a miscarriage and that's where that rumour must have come from. A miscarriage, that's it. Nothing more. As you can see I am able to conceive," said Shereece with a big smile on her face.

"They're beautiful," said Karen looking down at the babies. "Oh I'm so happy for you Shereece, I really am."

"Thank you."

"So who is the lucky fella?"

"Oh huh, he's at work at the moment. He's a doctor."

"Oh really. That's wonderful. Look at you eh, bagging the men with money," Karen said patting Shereece on her arm. They both laughed. "I'm just kidding Shereece."

"I know you are babe."

"I can't get over how gorgeous your babies are," said Karen as she looked down at the twins who were now kicking and moving their arms around.

"Thank you. So how are things over at the nursery?"

"Things are not great. You know a lot of parents removed their children from the nursery after April went missing. The trust levels went down to the pits. They're actually thinking of closing the nursery down," Karen told her sadly.

"Really?"

"Yeah I'm not kidding.... Poor April though. It's such a sick world we live in. I hope they catch whoever took her and kill them. No jail time just death."

"Yeah, you and me both. I've got to go. It was nice talking to you Karen." Shereece began pushing the buggy and took a few steps forward before Karen held her arm to stop her.

"Wait. Shereece are you ok? I know it must have been extra hard on you. You know with April and everything. You were really close to her. I hope you're ok."

"It was tough, but I've got my own babies to think about now. I can't live in the past. I hope some closure comes to April's parents."

"Yeah, yeah me too."

"Bye Karen." Karen stood still and watched Shereece walk away.

Detective Crease and Detective Mary are at the door of Kelly Tyler's mother's house. Kelly's mother reported Kelly missing after she failed to come home from the Triangle night club. Detective Mary rang the doorbell twice. Kelly's mother opened up the door until it caught on the latch and looked to see who it was.

"Hi there. We've come to speak to Miss Tyler," said Detective Crease.

"Yes that would be me," said Miss Tyler.

"Miss Tyler, I'm Detective Crease and this is my partner Detective Mary. We would like to talk to you about the missing person report you made for your daughter Kelly Tyler." Miss Tyler released the latch and fully opened the door.

"Yes, please come in." Detective Crease and Detective Mary both walked into the house and followed Miss Tyler as she led them into her living room

"Take a seat," said Miss Tyler. Detective Crease and Detective Mary sat down on the long grey linen sofa that was behind them while Miss Tyler sat on a grey armchair that was beside the two detectives. Miss Tyler was in her late forties, slim built with short blonde hair and wore glasses.

"So Miss Tyler, we will just need to take some simple details from you," said Detective Mary as she took out her note book and asked. "How old is your daughter Kelly?"

"She is twenty-three years old." Detective Mary jotted that down in her notebook and so did Detective Crease.

"Ok. Do you have any recent pictures of Kelly?" asked Detective Mary.

"Yes I do." Miss Tyler got up and took a small framed picture of Kelly off her living room wall. The picture was of Kelly standing alone in her mother's garden smiling. Miss Tyler handed the picture to Detective Mary. Detective Crease peered over the picture to also have a look at it.

"Lovely looking young lady," said Detective Mary.

"Yes she is. She's my only daughter. You need to find her," said Miss Tyler anxiously and teary eyed.

"That's why we're here Miss Tyler. We'll do our best," said Detective Crease.

"Miss Tyler, when was this picture taken?" asked Detective Mary.

"Around six months ago," replied Miss Tyler.

"Do you mind if we keep this picture?" asked Detective Crease.

"No, I don't mind. Keep it."

"Does Kelly live here with you?" asked Detective Mary.

"Yes she does. She's been living with me all her life."

"When was the last time you saw Kelly Miss Tyler?" asked Detective Mary.

"It was on July, July 27th, on a Friday evening. She said she was going to a night club in Bluendale called the Triangle."

"Did she leave directly from here?" asked Detective Crease.

"Yes, yes she did."

"Can you remember roughly what time in the evening?" asked Detective Mary.

"It was around 9ish, maybe 9.30."

"Did she go alone or with friends?" asked Detective Crease.

"She left here alone. Kelly doesn't really have friends. She likes to keep herself to herself."

"How about a boyfriend? Does she have one?" asked Detective Crease.

"No. Kelly revealed to me that she was a lesbian a few years back, so no boyfriend, and to my knowledge she doesn't have a girlfriend either."

"How close were you and Kelly?" asked Detective Mary.

"We were very close, very. She's my only child, that's why I know she would never just disappear without contacting me, especially for this long." Miss Tyler burst into tears. "I know something is wrong because she would have contacted me by now!" said Miss Tyler as she sobbed.

Detective Mary handed Miss Tyler a tissue from her pocket. Miss Tyler used the tissue to wipe away her tears.

"Sorry Miss Tyler. I know this must be hard," said Detective Mary sympathetically.

"Miss Tyler, do you have a partner?" asked Detective Crease.

"No, I'm single," replied Miss Tyler.

"Is Kelly's father in her life?" Detective Crease continued.

"Her father is not in Kelly's or mine. I don't know his whereabouts. He left me before Kelly was born and I haven't seen or heard from him since, neither has Kelly. He wasn't interested in being a father to her."

"So, there's no possibility she could be spending time with him?" asked Detective Crease.

"No! Did you not hear what I said? There's no way she's with her father. She would have told me if something like that were to happen. All her clothes are still in her bedroom. Don't you think she would have packed if she intended to stay somewhere else?!"

"Yes of course. Do you mind if we have a look in Kelly's bedroom?" asked Detective Crease.

"Sure, follow me," said Miss Tyler leading them upstairs to a large pink bedroom and switched on the light.

"This is my Kelly's bedroom," said Miss Tyler as she stood in the middle of it. The detectives scanned the bedroom walls noticing the big wall sticker which read *'To live would be a wonderful adventure,'* in red Italic writing.

"To live would be a wonderful adventure. I like that," said Detective Crease smiling as he read the sticker. Detective Mary looked at the pink bedding on her single bed.

"She loves the colour pink, doesn't she?" said Detective Mary smiling.

"Yes, it's her favourite colour," replied Miss Tyler.

Detective Crease switched his attention to Kelly's tall white wardrobe that was standing right beside Kelly's bed.

"Miss Tyler, we are just going to search Kelly's room, to see if there is any clue that might help us find her," said Detective Crease.

"I've gone through her things already and found nothing, but go ahead, I'll wait downstairs for you.

"Thank you," replied Detective Mary as Miss Tyler left the bedroom to wait in her living room.

After thoroughly searching Kelly's bedroom, the detectives came downstairs to the living room. As they entered the living room Miss Tyler looked up at them from her sofa.

"Well, you were right. We didn't find any clue that could lead us to Kelly's whereabouts," said Detective Crease.

"I did tell you," said Miss Tyler as both detectives sat back down on the sofa.

"Miss Tyler, can you think of any reason that Kelly may have had to just disappear?"

"No! Nothing like that happened! Something is wrong. I'm telling you both, me and Kelly have had many arguments in the past, but she has never reacted by cutting me off."

"Ok, how about her phone? What happens when you ring it?" asked Detective Crease.

"I first rung her phone the morning I woke up and realised she hadn't come back from the club. It just went straight to voicemail, and it's been going to voicemail ever since."

"Can we have her mobile number please?" asked Detective Mary.

"Yes." Miss Tyler took her phone out of her pocket and scrolled to Kelly's number in her contacts and passed the phone to Detective Mary.

"Thank you," said Detective Mary. Detective Mary and Detective Crease jotted down Kelly's mobile number in their notebooks.

"Does Kelly work Miss Tyler?" asked Detective Crease.

"No. She was in college studying beauty therapy. I've contacted her college and they said she hasn't been in since July 27th, the same day she went to the night club."

"What college is she enrolled with?" asked Detective Crease.

"Bluendale College," replied Miss Tyler. Detective Crease jotted that information down in his notebook.

"So, this night club she went to, the Triangle, does she go there regularly?" asked Detective Crease.

"Yes, she usually goes every other week at least."

"By herself?" asked Detective Mary.

"Yes. It's a lesbian night club. She goes there to let her hair down, and also I think to meet someone who could potentially be her partner."

"Tell us a bit more about Kelly's character. Was she confident? Outspoken?" asked Detective Crease.

"My Kelly's not really a confident girl. She's quite insecure. I don't know why because she's so beautiful, but she's insecure and can be quite vulnerable. I always said to her that she shouldn't be clubbing on her own, but she always insisted to me that she'll be ok. Sometimes I even suggested going with her, but she shut me down every time. She didn't fancy going clubbing with her mother," Miss Tyler smiled sadly.

"Miss Tyler. Is there anything else you can tell us that you think might help us with this investigation?" asked Detective Crease.

"Please go to the Triangle night club," said Miss Tyler eagerly.

"Oh, don't worry, we're going to do that," replied Detective Crease.

"I tried to contact them, but they told me they couldn't give out confidential information to the public," said Miss Tyler.

"Yes they would say that. It's club policy," said Detective Mary.

"The Triangle nightclub is going to be the first place on our list in search for your daughter Miss Tyler," said Detective Crease. Both detectives then stood up.

"Thank you for your cooperation Miss Tyler," said Detective Mary as she reached out her hand. Miss Tyler stood up and shook both Detective Mary and Detective Crease's hands.

"If you hear anything regarding your daughter, or if she should turn up, please contact us right away," said Detective Crease as he handed Miss Tyler a contact card.

"Yes, yes I will do," said Miss Tyler as she took the card. Both Detectives then walked out of Miss Tyler's house. As the detectives got to the garden gate, Miss Tyler called out to them from her front door.

"Detectives!" Both Detectives turned around. "You will bring her back to me, won't you?!" said Miss Tyler clearly worried.

"We'll do everything we can," replied Detective Mary. Then both detectives walked out of the garden, got into their vehicle and drove off.

"What time exactly did Kelly Tyler enter and leave your night club?" asked Detective Mary to Brian McDonald, the night club owner of the Triangle.

All three of them, Detective Crease, Detective Mary and Brian McDonald were seated in Brian's office within the nightclub. The detectives had contacted the club in advance to arrange a meeting with the club owner to discuss Kelly Tyler's disappearance.

"She came in at 10.20pm," said Brian.

"And this was on Friday July 27th?" asked Detective Crease.

"Yes that's right."

"How are you able to confirm this information?" asked Detective Crease.

"It's all here," said Brian as he tapped his hand on a computer monitor that was on his office table.

"Everybody that comes to my night club has to have their photo ID scanned at the door before entry. Kelly Tyler scanned hers in at 10.20pm on Friday July 27th."

"Can I have a look at that?" asked Detective Crease referring to the monitor.

"Yeah sure." Detective Crease got up and walked round to Brian's side of the table to face the monitor.

"Do you also have CCTV footage of her entering your club?" asked Detective Crease inquisitively.

"Yes, I believe I do. You know when you contacted me about the dates and times, I went through my CCTV footage and saw what appears to be her," said Brian as he clicked on the camera gallery on his monitor with his mouse. He went to the camera footage that was monitoring his night club door on Friday July 27th. He sped up the camera to 10.20pm and there Kelly Tyler was, taking her ID out of her hand bag.

"That her? Looks like her judging by her photo ID," said Brian.

"Pause it," said Detective Crease. Brian paused the camera while Kelly was looking up. You could see her face from a bird's eye view.

Detective Mary came around the table to also have a look at the footage.

"Mary have you got that picture on you?" asked Detective Crease.

"Yes," said Detective Mary before taking out the picture of Kelly Tyler. Detective Mary stared hard at the paused camera footage of Kelly Tyler. She then looked at the picture, then looked back at Kelly Tyler's face on the monitor.

"Yep, that definitely looks like her to me," said Detective Mary. After looking at the picture and looking at the monitor, Detective Crease agreed it was Kelly Tyler in the camera footage.

"Yes that's her alright. Ok, keep playing the footage," said Detective Crease. Brian resumed playing the CCTV footage. On the footage you could see Kelly Tyler getting her ID scanned then walk into the club on her own. "Were there any incidents in the club that night? Any fights or acts of violence?" asked Detective Mary.

"No, none whatsoever. Look I understand you guys are looking for this missing young lady, and I'll help as much as I can, but I don't think you'll find any links to her going missing here. I run a respectable night club and we hardly ever have any trouble," said Brian.

"The thing is, she went missing the same night she came to your club, so you must understand why we must investigate here," said Detective Mary.

"Yes sure, I understand that," said Brian as he scratched his head.

"Moving along, can you get us footage of Kelly Tyler leaving your club?" said Detective Crease to Brian.

"I can try. It may take forever though."

"We have time," replied Detective Crease.

Brian sighed and said, "Ok". He then went to a camera on his monitor that showed a bird's eye view of his night club door.

"So, from this camera we can see at least some of the faces of people leaving my club. As I said we could be here for hours detectives. My night club starts at 9pm and closes at 3am. All there is to do now is sit down and watch the footage. You know you both can go and come back and I'll let you both know if I can recognise her leaving," Brian offered as he looked at both detectives. Both detectives glanced at each other for a second.

"No, that won't be necessary Brian. Will be just fine here," said Detective Crease.

"Alright," replied Brian shaking his head. Both Detectives took chairs and sat beside Brian to view the the monitor.

"How long have you had this night club Brian?" asked Detective Crease.

"Coming up to eight years now," said Brian.

"Good business?" asked Detective Crease.

"Hey I'm not complaining," said Brian. Detective Crease smiled.

Several hours went by while both Detectives and Brian were watching the night club CCTV footage. Then suddenly Detective Crease said to stop the footage. He leaned into the monitor.

"Isn't that her there?" said Detective Crease as he pointed at what appeared to be Kelly Tyler leaving the night club with Shereece. Brian zoomed in on the footage. You could see the side of Kelly Tyler's face clearly after he zoomed in.

"Yep that's her, leaving at 2.30am. Who's that holding her hand?" asked Detective Mary.

"Brian can you zoom in on her face?" Detective Crease requested as he pointed his finger on Shereece's body. Brian zoomed in on Shereece's face.

"Oh my God. You know who that is don't you Mary?" said Detective Crease. Both detectives were shocked to see Shereece holding hands with Kelly Tyler. They were now in no doubt that Shereece was connected with every one of their missing person cases.

"Am I missing something here?" said Brian as he looked at both detectives.

"Please, look up the name Shereece Corret on your monitor and see what time she entered your club that night. Can you do that for us please?" said Detective Mary to Brian. Brian did as he was asked. Typing away on his keyboard, he brought up Shereece's photo ID. Her ID came up on the monitor screen.

"There you go. She came in at 11.55pm, see, says so right here," said Brian as he pointed on the monitor where it showed the time Shereece checked in.

"Brian, we are going to need the camera footage we've been going through today," said Detective Crease.

"Yeah sure, I can burn it off on a disc for you."

"Brian McDonald, thank you for your patience and cooperation. You've been very helpful," said Detective Crease.

"Oh no problem. I hope you find the lady," said Brian.

Meanwhile Shereece was at home bathing the babies when she got a text message on her phone. She looked at her phone. The message was from Freddy.

'Hi', the message read. Shereece ignored the message, put her phone back on the corner of the bath tub and continued to bathe Shyla and Peree. Then her phone started ringing. She looked at her phone and could see it was Freddy calling. She answered the call.

"What do you want?" asked Shereece annoyed.

"I just want to see how you are."

"I'm fine, goodbye," Shereece said abruptly.

"No no don't go," said Freddy eager to keep Shereece on the phone.

"Look, I'm in the middle of something right now," Shereece said as she sighed, wishing Freddy would just get off the phone.

"What are you doing?" asked Freddy trying to keep Shereece on the phone.

"I'm bathing my twins if you must know," replied Shereece irritably.

"Well let me call you back when you're done."

"For what?" asked Shereece.

"Look, I've been thinking about you since that night. I'm sorry for the way I acted. I'm not used to women having their way with me like that. You know I would like us to see each other again, all on your terms."

"Hmmm, what about all that stuff you said when I was leaving your house?"

"I was upset. I was just talking out my arse. I didn't mean any of it, trust me. Can we please just put that all behind us and start over, so you can get to know me more as a person?"

"You need to understand one thing, if you're going to rock with me, I wear the trousers, not the other way round," Shereece explained bluntly.

"Understood," said Freddy enjoying the satisfaction of being put in his place. He wasn't used to dating such a dominant woman, and as pissed off as he was, when Shereece had her way with him, in hindsight it turned him on.

"Good. In that case, maybe I'll give you a call later. Maybe!" said Shereece taunting him on purpose.

"Oh come on Shereece-" bleep. Shereece ended the call, finished bathing the babies and then took them into her bedroom. After dressing them she sat down on the carpet to play with them.

Five minutes later she got up off the floor and sat on her armchair, leaving the babies on the carpet. She got on her phone and called Victor.

Shereece had decided earlier on in the week that Victor would have to kill his brother Mark as a sacrifice to Satan, as Victor and his brother were very close. Victor tried to offer a cousin of his as a sacrifice instead of his brother, but Shereece was adamant that it must be the brother.

The lust and infatuation both slaves had for Shereece made Victor agree. The influence she had over them was so overwhelming that they would do anything to serve her.

Victor's phone rang three times before he answered, "Hello Mistress Lilith."

"Where are you?" asked Shereece getting straight to the point.

"I'm at my brother's flat."

"You know tonight is your final initiation night, don't you?"

"Yes Mistress, I know," replied Victor nervously.

"And you're ready?" Victor took a deep breath before saying, "Yes...yes Mistress I'm ready."

"Say it. Say tonight I'm going to sacrifice my brother."

"Tonight I'm going to sacrifice my brother," said Victor after a short pause.

"Where is he now?" asked Shereece curiously.

"He's in his front room watching football Mistress."

"And where are you?"

"I'm in the back garden. He can't hear me talking," replied Victor.

"Good. So we're going stick to the plan ok. Lure him here for 9pm exactly."

"Ok Mistress. 9pm exact, I'm going to bring him to yours."

"See you then," said Shereece before ending the call. Victor put his phone in his pocket and walked into his brother's flat. He entered the front room where Mark was watching football.

"Hey Mark," Victor greeted his brother.

"Shush, not now Vic. We're 2:1 down. I can't believe this. Come on Chelsea you got to beat Arsenal for this cup!" said Mark loudly as he punched the air in frustration.

Victor sat down beside Mark. Mark was a 37-year old, good looking guy with a slim build and well-groomed blonde hair. He worked as a personal assistant in an IT company. He loved football, going to the pub and women.

"Mark, one second. Remember I told you about that girl?"

"What girl? Come on Chelsea!" Mark screamed at the TV as a Chelsea player took a strike at the goal.

"The girl I told you about that I met online. The girl that wanted the threesome."

"Oh yeah, what about her?" Mark giggled while his eyes were still fixated on his television.

"Well, she wants to meet tonight at 9pm at her house. She wants us to fuck her brains out bro," Victor said smiling.

"What do you mean us? She hasn't even seen or met me."

"She's a freak Mark, this is what I'm telling you. I've been speaking to her for over a month now. I sent her a picture of you and she's like-"

"Wait what? You sent her a pic of me? Where did you get the nerve to do that without asking my permission?" Mark said abruptly as he turned to face Victor.

"Forget all that Mark, this is kinky pussy on the plate."

"Let me see a picture of her." Victor went into his phone picture gallery and pulled up one of the many pictures he had of Shereece.

This particular picture was of Shereece posing in a Latex dress with her hands on her hips staring at the camera in a seductive manner. Victor showed the picture to Mark.

"Fucking hell! Look at the gunners on her. She's a body builder. She's got more muscles than me," said Mark in astonishment.

"Hot, isn't she?" said Victor.

"Yeah if you're gay. Might as well be fucking a bloke. I'm not interested Vic. You can keep your manly looking women to yourself," said Mark as turned back to the TV.

"Ahhh come on Mark. If you don't come she won't see me. She said you're lovely looking and I don't get to have sex with her without you being involved," stressed Victor.

"You're a tosser Vic. You shouldn't have got me involved in this. I never told you to send her my picture. Plus she's a nigger. I don't fuck niggers."

"Come on Mark, let's not be racist here. You telling me you've never shagged a black or mixed raced girl before?"

"Nope, never have. It's against my principles," said Mark firmly.

"Come on Mark, just take one for the team. Do it for me. It will be fun."

"Look Vic, it might be different if she wasn't so muscular, that's a turn off for me."

"Aren't you the one that always used to say you'll try anything once?"

Mark laughed. "Yeah well not this once."

Victor put his arm around Mark's shoulder and literally begged him to come.

"Come on Mark please. I've got to fuck this broad. You've got to come."

"Why are you so attracted to her?" said Mark with genuine curiosity.

"Because she's different, besides, not everybody's got the good looks you've got. I haven't been laid in like forever." Mark giggled. "Don't laugh, it isn't funny. It's been a while Mark." Mark sighed.

"You're not going to let me out of this one, are you?"

"No I'm not. Come on, you're my brother. Take one for the team," said Victor as he shook Mark's shoulder. Mark sighed again then looked Victor in the eyes.

"You owe me," said Mark.

9pm came fast. Mark pulled up to Shereece's house after following the address that Victor had given him. Mark parked in a free parking space then turned the ignition off.

"Can't believe you talked me into this," said Mark.

"You'll thank me after Mark. Don't worry, we're going to have fun trust me." Victor went on his phone and messaged Shereece to tell her he was outside.

"You haven't even told me this woman's name," said Mark.

"Lilith," Victor told him.

"Lilith?"

"Yeah, that's her name, Lilith." Victor went on his phone again and messaged Shereece. 'I can't call you Mistress in front of my brother because he will think that's weird. I'm just going to call you Lilith.' 'Understood. I'm coming to the door now,' replied Shereece. Shereece came to her front door and opened it.

"Is that her there?" asked Mark as he pointed to Shereece who was standing in her doorway with the corridor light on wearing a black dressing gown.

"Yes, that's her," said Victor. Victor opened up his passenger seat door and exited the car. Mark did the same and then locked the car. They walked towards Shereece's house. When they got to Shereece's door, Victor greeted her.

"Hi Lilith," said Victor as he reached his hand out to Shereece for her to shake. Shereece shook Victor's hand as if she'd never met him before.

"How are you Victor? Nice to meet you in person," said Shereece as she smiled. "And hello there handsome. Mark, right?" asked Shereece as she turned to Mark.

"Yeah Mark. That's my name." Shereece put her hand out for Mark to shake. Mark shook Shereece's hand briefly.

"Well, come in," said Shereece as she ushered Mark and Victor into her house before closing and locking the door. Shereece then walked past both the brothers and into her living room, telling them to follow her.

"Nice place you have here," said Mark after looking around Shereece's living room.

"Thank you. You guys take a seat." Victor and Mark sat on Shereece's sofa. "What can I get you both to drink? I have Courvoisier, E&J or Malibu, take your pick," said Shereece smiling.

"I'm fine. I've got to drive back home so don't really want to be drinking," said Mark.

"Ahhh don't be such a boring git. One glass isn't going to hurt you," said Shereece. Mark looked at Victor.

"She's right Mark. A glass of whisky isn't gonna hurt nobody. I'll have a glass of Courvoisier mixed with coke if you have that please," said Victor.

"Yes I do have that." Shereece then looked at Mark as if to see if he had changed his mind about having a drink.

"Oh go on then. I'll have the same," said Mark.

"Great," said Shereece before leaving the room. Mark turned to Victor and whispered, "Not my type." Victor whispered back, "Take one for the team."

Shereece made the drinks in the kitchen, making sure to slip Rohypnol into the glass that she prepared for Mark.

"Here you go boys," said Shereece as she gave Victor and Mark their drinks.

"Thank you," said Victor and Mark simultaneously.

"Now I'm going to make myself a drink. I'll be back in a second," said Shereece as she headed back to her kitchen.

She poured herself a glass of coke, came back to the living room and sat down on a chair beside the brothers.

"So, Mark, tell me about yourself. I know everything about your brother, I know nothing about you. What do you do with yourself?"

"I work as a PA in an IT company," said Mark proudly.

"Oh nice. Sounds fancy. Where's it based?"

"In Epping. Our office is based in Epping."

"Cool. I'm not too familiar with Epping."

"It's a nice place. Nice and quiet down there."

"Ok," said Shereece as Mark took a sip of his drink.

"So, what about you? What do you do with yourself?" asked Mark.

"I'm a dominatrix." The surprise made Mark splutter on the drink he was drinking before saying, "A what?"

"A dominatrix!" Shereece repeated bluntly. There was a brief silence in the room before Victor started giggling.

Then Mark looked at his brother and started laughing. Shereece took a sip of her drink while looking at Mark.

What's so funny?" asked Shereece.

"Are you serious? Are you really a dominatrix? Like those women who dress up in latex and whip men and shit?" asked Mark.

"Is that the stereotype then? There's much more to it than that," said Shereece.

"Oh my gosh. Vic what have you got me into," said Mark as he took another sip of his drink.

"Don't worry, I won't be whipping you," said Shereece.

"I sure hope not," replied Mark.

"You are one handsome chap aren't you, Mark?" said Shereece.

"Thank you, thank you for that comment." Mark took a look at Victor's drink on the dining table and could see the glass was still full.

"Vic, what's the matter with you? You haven't taken a sip of your drink," said Mark.

"Oh, I just got carried away listening to you two talk. I forgot it was there," said Victor as he picked up his drink and took a heavy sip.

Shereece turned on her TV with her remote control. The channel 4 news popped up on the screen. The bulletin read MISSIING APRIL.

"Still no trace of missing April after 18 months. Police and detectives are saying they will not give up the search until they find her," said the news reporter.

"What a sick world it is," said Shereece.

"Yes, sick indeed. She's definitely dead," said Mark.

"What makes you so sure?" asked Shereece.

"Got to be. Some pervert's killed her and gotten rid of the body. That's what these child molesters do, don't they? It's the nursery's fault though."

"Why is it the nursery's fault?" asked Victor.

"What? Haven't you been following the case? She went missing on a nursery trip. Somebody kidnapped her while the nursery was on an outing. That's fucking wrong that is. Somebody should have been watching her. That nursery should be closed down I don't care what anybody says." Mark spoke these words with a passion.

"I didn't know that," said Victor.

"Well, I don't know if we should be so quick to blame the nursery. Maybe whoever took her was just so good at what they do that it just went completely unnoticed," said Shereece.

"Nah, no excuses. Somebody should have had an eye on that kid. It's a nursery. The kids should be monitored at all times," said Mark.

"Yeah maybe you're right. Well, the parents are suing the nursery," said Shereece.

"Are they? Good. Sue them and close it down!" said Mark sternly.

"Let's not spoil the mood with all this," said Shereece as she turned the channel over. She turned the channel to the sex station Television x. Two women were having sex in the 69 position.

"Are you into lesbian porn Mark?" asked Shereece. "I already know Victor is."

"Yes I am," agreed Victor.

"Yeah I love it," said Mark. Shereece walked over to Mark and began rubbing his chest. She then leaned forward towards Mark's face in an attempt to kiss him on the lips. Mark turned his face to the side making Shereece miss his lips and said, "Sorry, I'm not into kissing."

Shereece stood up with her legs apart right in front of Mark. She undid her dressing gown and let it fall to the floor baring her nude body.

"What are you into then?" asked Shereece. Mark looked Shereece's body up and down. He started seeing double of her and his vision blurred.

"I think I've had too much, too much to drink," Mark stuttered. His eyes became drowsy.

"Oh don't be silly baby. You've only had one glass," said Shereece as she smiled. Mark turned to Victor.

"Vic, I think we should go now," said Mark. Victor's eyes teared up. His conscience started to kick in. The realisation of him actually killing his own brother started to sink in.

"It's ok Mark. Everything is going to be ok," said Victor as he rubbed Mark's shoulder. Shereece got on top of Mark, putting her legs either side of his waist. Her bare arse was on his lap. Mark raised his right hand to Shereece's right breast and groped it.

"Don't be afraid hun, I won't bite," said Shereece seductively. Shereece's words echoed in Mark's ear and had a distorted tone.

"Something's not right. Get off me bitch!" said Mark out loud as he pushed Shereece off him. He quickly got up off the sofa but fell straight to the ground as he tried to walk. He managed to turn onto his back and vaguely saw Victor and Shereece looking down at him.

Shereece started giggling. She then bent down towards Mark and whispered, "You're our sacrifice tonight Mark. Farewell."

Then she looked at Victor and said, "Bring him down." Mark was now only semiconscious. Shereece opened up her basement trap door and Victor carried Mark down the basement stairs. Shereece followed them down closing the trapdoor after her.

When they got down there, Ricky was waiting on his knees, just outside the centre of the basement behind a large circle of candles.

He was naked and had his eyes closed. In the circle of the candles was a large pentagram drawn by Shereece.

"You know what to do," said Shereece. Carrying Mark on his shoulders, Victor stepped over the candles and put Mark's body on top of the pentagon star.

Shereece pulled out her Rambo knife and extended it to Victor. Victor took the knife from Shereece. They stared into each other's eyes.

"You know what you've got to do," said Shereece. Victor looked at Mark's helpless body on the floor. He then got on his knees and raised the Rambo knife in his right hand into the air and aimed it at Mark's chest. Victor's hand which was holding the knife started shaking. He stalled.

"What are you waiting for Victor? Do it now!" shouted Shereece. Victor took his eyes off of Mark and looked at Ricky whose eyes were now open.

"Do it Victor, do it. I did mine, now it's your turn. Hail Satan! Hail Satan!" said Ricky out loud. Victor looked back at his brother's face. He started to sob.

"I can't do it, I can't. He's my brother. Wake up Mark let's go!" said Victor as he dropped the knife on the floor and began to shake Mark's body.

"What the fuck are you doing? How dare you disobey your Mistress. Pick up that knife and kill him!" Shereece shouted.

"NO! I'm going to the police! This is all wrong!" Victor shouted back. Shereece began angrily huffing and puffing. She ran to her box of weapons and took out her Beretta handgun and pointed the gun at Victor's head.

"Kill him or I'll kill you." Victor looked down the barrel of the handgun.

"Victor you traitor! Mistress just kill him, we can't trust him to leave, he'll turn us both in," said Ricky.

Shereece looked at Ricky. As soon as she took her eyes off Victor, Victor slapped the handgun out of her hand and dashed for the basement stairs. Shereece ran for the gun, picked it up and ran after Victor.

Victor was halfway up the stairs when Shereece aimed her gun at his back and unloaded three shots. All three shots hit their mark. The shots shook Victor's body before he came tumbling down the steps, his body landing at Shereece's feet.

Shereece pointed the gun at Victor's forehead and pulled the trigger, blowing his brains out. She then walked up to Mark who was still laid out on the pentagram helplessly and pointed the Beretta at his head before pulling the trigger. The bullet blew half of Mark's skull off, killing him instantly. Blood splattered on Ricky's face and body. Ricky's body shook, scared from the gun blast.

"What a mess I'm going to have to clean up. Why didn't you help me catch him?!" Shereece screamed at Ricky.

"You told me I must be on my knees until you tell me to move Mistress."

"You idiot. Imagine if he would have gotten away."

"He would have never gotten away Mistress. Satan is protecting us." Shereece turned to her right, facing her wall of coffins.

"Tonight was fucked up. Victor that fucking pussy punked out on me. Now it's just the two of us, well, with the exception of Kia."

"I'm all you need Mistress; I'll never betray you. I'll always be obedient to you my Goddess."

Shereece turned to Ricky and brushed her gun across the side of his cheek roughly.

"I know you will Ricky, I have faith in you." She then got on her knees and began to take off Mark's shirt.

"Looks like I'm going to have to sacrifice Mark instead." She picked her Rambo knife up, lifted it into the air and plunged it into Mark's chest. She sliced Mark's chest open and dragged out his heart with her bare hand.

Blood soaked her whole right arm. She sliced the heart open with the knife and then squeezed it over her face yelling, "Hail Satan!"

Ricky started to chant "Hail Satan" with her. She squeezed the heart over Ricky's head. Blood gushed over the top of Ricky's head and face. "Hail Satan! Hail Satan!" they both chanted.

Chapter 16

New Recruit

It was 9 o'clock in the morning. A day after Shereece had slain Victor and Mark.

"Wake up Kia, it's time to be fed," said Shereece as she sat beside Kia's open coffin. Kia woke up.

"What time is it?" Kia asked yawning.

"Its 9am. Time for you to eat. I've made you scrambled eggs, sausages and toast."

"How are the babies?" asked Kia concerned.

"They're good. I not long ago changed their nappies."

"And you've fed them?"

"Yes, of course I've fed them," said Shereece in annoyance.

"Where are they?"

"Where do you think they are Kia? They're in my room. You know that's where they stay. Now open up." Shereece fed Kia a fork full of scrambled eggs.

I heard gunshots last night. I was frightened. What happened?" Shereece went quiet for a few seconds, looking Kia in her eyes before answering.

"I had to kill one of my slaves, and his brother."

"What? Why?" said Kia shocked.

"My slave betrayed me. It was his initiation, his turn to make a sacrifice to our Lord Satan. He chickened out, tried to run out on me and I couldn't have that. He was supposed to sacrifice his brother."

"His own brother?" asked Kia visibly surprised.

"Yes. For my slaves to prove their ultimate loyalty to me, I order them to kill somebody close to them."

"Wow."

"I take my beliefs seriously Kia," Shereece stressed. "You said you want to be involved; did you really mean it?" asked Shereece intensely.

"Yes I meant it, but what will be in it for me?"

"If you kill for me, if you make a sacrifice, I will trust you, I will allow you to be free from your coffin, free for us to raise our babies together."

Kia could hear the sincerity in Shereece's voice. These were the words she wanted to hear, an opportunity to finally be free.

"Then I'm in. No bullshitting Shereece, I will do it, tonight, I'll even do it tonight," said Kia confidently. Shereece smiled and chuckled.

"You really sound eager."

"That's because I'm serious. I won't let you down Shereece, I swear on the babies."

"You can't let me down because I'll kill you if you do. If you flop, if I give you someone to kill and you back out last minute, then I'll kill you Kia, I mean it. I'm getting tired of looking after you. You won't be of use to me if you're not part of my cult."

Kia knew Shereece meant what she said and it frightened her. 'Imagine I'm not able to go through with it,' she thought. 'She really will kill me.'

"I hear you and understand Shereece. I won't flop."

"Good. I'm going to record the whole thing. The sacrifice you make will be recorded, so if you do think about going to the police once you have your freedom, or running away from me, I'll show police the video of you committing a murder." Kia froze.

She wasn't expecting that response. She now knew if she went through with the human sacrifice she would never be free from Shereece, but at this point she was willing to do anything to have some form of freedom and to be with her babies.

"That's fine. I have no issues with that," said Kia, trying to sound confident.

"Who will the sacrifice be?" Kia asked.

"I have somebody in mind. A man I dated, or I could give you one of my clients."

"Any, I don't care," said Kia determinedly. Shereece smiled.

"I'm loving your attitude Kia. Let me think about it. For now finish off your food, it's getting cold."

After feeding Kia, Shereece went to see to the babies. They were both fast asleep in their cot. She sat in her armchair and rocked back and forth in it, thinking of who she should have Kia kill. Shereece wondered. She got out her phone and called Freddy. He answered after two rings.

"I knew you'd come around," said Freddy smugly at the other end of the line.

"I see you're still full of yourself," replied Shereece.

"I'm just playing with you baby. How are you?"

"I'm good, just minding my babies."

"Cool cool. Listen Shereece, I'm actually at work at the moment, but can I call you back say around 6.30?"

"Well actually I just wanted to know if you were free this evening?"

"Yeah, yes I am, why? Do you want to meet up or something?" Freddy asked with enthusiasm.

"If you're up for it."

"Yeah I'm up for that. Where are we meeting and what time?"

"8.30 at my place."

"Oh, ok, ok that's cool. I'll bring a bottle of wine with me."

"Just bring yourself and don't be late. I'll text you my address."

"Ok Shereece, I'll be on time, don't worry about that."

"Good." Then Shereece hung up the phone.

"I've got to fuck her tonight," said Freddy to himself.

After coming off the phone, Shereece went down to the basement. She opened Kia's coffin and began to brief her about her plans. "Tonight 8.30 he'll be here."

"Who will?" Kia asked confused.

"The man you're going to sacrifice."

"Who is he?"

"He's just some arsehole I dated."

Kia started to get scared. Her heart began to race. She didn't know if she could actually go through with it.

"Don't you think maybe I should learn more about the religion first, then do it? Let me read some of the Satan bible you have, then do it."

"No! We don't have time for that right now," Shereece snapped.

"You'll do this first and then you can read it Kia, don't try to back out now. You gave me your word that you were ready so don't you dare back out on me now," Shereece warned. "This is your ticket to your freedom remember? You know what I do to people who back out on me. Please don't make me have to kill my own sister because I will do it if I have to," Shereece said aggressively. "I really want you to be part of this thing Kia. You'll see how good life is for you once you join the cult."

Kia steeled herself for the task ahead.

"Ok Shereece, set it up. But you give me your word that after this sacrifice, you'll free me?"

"You have my word Kia, but first hear this. You and Derrick have come up on the news as a missing couple. What will you tell people who ask you where Derrick is and where you've both been?"

"I'll come up with something. I'll say we were in a car accident or something."

"Then you'll still have to explain where Derrick's body is. And you'll have to explain where you've been."

Kia thought for a moment before replying, "I'll say it's in the lake somewhere. I'll say we crashed and slid into a lake. I'll make up something good. What did you do with his car? Is it still parked outside?"

"No. I torched it a long time ago. It's funny you mentioned a lake because that's where I pushed the car into after burning it.

"You see, the story will go together well."

"Not totally Kia. People will want to know where you've been. The police and your friends. This is what you'll say. Derrick cheated on you with another woman. You broke up and haven't seen him since. You moved to Scotland to stay with your auntie because you just wanted to flee and recover from the heartache of your break up. You left everything behind. You got in contact with me and heard I had twin baby girls. And that's why you came back, to spend time with your nieces. That's going to be the basis of your story. It's something we'll have to put together well before you can leave here."

"I understand Shereece. I'll say whatever needs to be said." Shereece stroked Kia's cheek as she said, "You do know how you're going to kill him right? You're going to stab him to death with the same knife you used to stab me."

"Shereece I'm scared, I'm actually scared," Kia said in panic.

"Don't be. You'll do fine, you've got it in you, I have a scar on my leg to prove it."

They both chuckled. Shereece stared into Kia's eyes before leaning into her face for a kiss. Kia didn't budge, she met Shereece's lips and they kissed passionately. Shereece's doorbell started ringing, interrupting the kiss.

"Who the fuck is that?" said Shereece. She looked in her monitor that showed the camera to the front door. "Oh fuck. What do they want now?" said Shereece.

"Who is it?" asked Kia.

"Nobody important. Just relax, I'll take care of it." Shereece closed Kia's coffin and climbed up the basement stairs. The doorbell rang two more times.

"I'm coming!" said Shereece out loud in frustration. She opened her front door. It was Detective Crease and Detective Mary.

"Hi there Shereece. We meet again," said Detective Crease with a smile on his face.

"How can I help you? I've told you everything I know about April."

"Where not here about April Shereece, we're here about Kelly Tyler," said Detective Mary.

"Who is that?" asked Shereece looking bewildered. Both detectives glanced at each other then looked back at Shereece.

"Shereece Corret, we would like you to come down to the station with us to answer some questions," said Detective Crease.

"Am I under arrest?"

"No you're not but-"

"Then I'm not going anywhere," said Shereece swiftly cutting off Detective Crease.

"Why not Shereece?" asked Detective Mary.

"Shereece where were you on the night of Friday July 27th?" asked Detective Crease.

"I don't know where I was on July 27th Friday night, that was ages ago. How am I supposed to remember? Why are you guys harassing me?"

"Shereece, we've got you on camera leaving the Triangle nightclub with a young lady named Kelly Tyler. Now Kelly Tyler has been reported missing. You wouldn't know anything about that would you?" asked Detective Crease.

"I don't have any idea about anybody going missing. I sometimes go to Triangle nightclub when I'm horny and looking for a quick fuck. I don't remember the names of everybody I fuck detectives, so maybe I did leave a nightclub with a lady named Kelly, but I haven't got anything to do with her going missing," said Shereece.

The detectives were taken back by Shereece's aggressive response.

"Let's cut the bullshit Shereece. We know you're Mistress Lilith, a dominatrix. Why is it that people who are associated with you wind up disappearing? We know you're responsible for the disappearance of Kelly Tyler, Stuart Green, and little April. What are you? Some kind of serial killer or something? What have you done with their bodies Shereece?" asked Detective Crease bluntly.

"You two can both go to hell!" replied Shereece before attempting to close the door. Detective Crease caught the door with his foot.

"Look, if you say you're innocent then fine. Let us just come in and take a look around," said Detective Crease.

"Just a brief look Shereece," said Detective Mary.

"After accusing me of being a serial killer? How dare you! I haven't killed anybody. You guys have already looked around my house, and found nothing. I have nothing to hide. Now if I'm not under arrest I would appreciate it if you both left my property, now!"

Detective Crease released his foot from the door.

"We will be back. Come on Mary, we've got work to do," said Detective Crease as he pinched his hat and nodded to Shereece.

Shereece slammed her front door shut, then leaned her back on it staring up at her ceiling. Her mind began to spin. She started to think about her date with Freddy later that night. 'Things are getting hot. Maybe I should call it off. How the fuck do they know I'm Mistress Lilith?' she thought to herself. She started to hear the babies crying so she ran upstairs to their room.

"Hey my little munchkins, mummy is here. No need to cry. Come here," said Shereece before picking up both babies. She held one in each arm. They eventually stopped crying.

"Is that all you wanted ha, for mummy to pick you up?" She then put them into their baby carriers and went downstairs to the basement. Shereece opened Kia's coffin.

"Hi Shereece. Awww, my babies. Oh my God they're getting so big. Can I hold them?" asked Kia full of emotion as she saw her two babies.

Shereece helped lean Kia up. She took Peree outside of her baby carrier and placed her into Kia's arms.

"Please Shereece, take off the handcuffs. I want to hold her properly. I promise I won't try to fight you. I'm done with all that now. I want to be with you not fight you."

Shereece looked Kia in her eyes then went into her purse and took out the key for the handcuffs. She then used them to unlock Kia's handcuffs.

"Thank you Shereece. Awww look at you Peree," said Kia as she held Peree up in the air. Peree smiled. "She's so gorgeous. You're so gorgeous, aren't you baby? Yes you are," said Kia twisting and turning Peree in the air. Tears started to flow down Kia's cheeks. She began sobbing. "My gosh. She's so beautiful. Can I hold Shyla too?"

Shereece took Shyla out of her baby carrier and handed her to Kia.

"Be careful you don't drop them," said Shereece.

"I won't," replied Kia. Kia started rocking both the babies in her arms. She was so happy to see her twins after what seemed to be such a long time.

"Kia, I have to talk to you about tonight."

"What? what's wrong?" Kia asked wary of what she was going to hear next.

"We're going to have to call it off."

"Why?" asked Kia surprised.

"It was the police at the door Kia. They know about me. They know about the killings, and it won't be long before they come to the basement and find the bodies," said Shereece looking at the coffins containing the bodies of her victims.

"How do they know?" Kia was feeling mixed emotions about hearing what Shereece was telling her. Part of Kia was feeling excited at the thought of police coming to free her and her babies, but another part of her was frightened that Shereece would kill her before the police would get a chance to get to her.

"I don't know how they know they just do!" snapped Shereece. Kia responded the way she thought best.

"Shereece, let me make the sacrifice to prove my loyalty, then we can both leave together with our babies. I have sixty thousand in my bank account. We can leave the country."

"Money is not a problem. I have enough of that," said Shereece rubbing her fingers together. "The thing is, we can't leave this property."

"Why not?" asked Kia confused.

"Because we can't alright we can't, and I'm not going to jail."

"So, what's going to happen with me then Shereece? Are you still going to free me?"

"You can't be free until you make your sacrifice."

"But you said you're calling it off!" Kia exclaimed. Shereece sighed.

"Ok, I'll do it. I'll bring you your first human sacrifice. What was I thinking? I'm not going to get caught. My faith must be weakening for me to even think I could get caught. My Lord Satan will never allow that to happen. The sacrifice will go on tonight. Are you sure you're ready Kia?"

"Yes I'm ready. Let's do it," said Kia trying to sound confident. Shereece got on her phone and texted Freddy her home address. 'I'll see you at 8.30 honey,' Freddy texted back.

"Come on. Let me take the babies now," said Shereece as she reached for Shyla and Peree. "Today might be your last day in this coffin," Shereece said before closing the coffin lid on Kia.

Shereece spent the day looking after the babies in her living room and watching TV. By 7pm she had put the babies to bed. It was now 8.30pm and Freddy had not yet arrived. Shereece called Freddy from her phone. Freddy's phone rang three times before he picked up.

"Hi baby," said Freddy.

"Where are you?" asked Shereece sharply.

"I'm on my way. There's just a little bit of traffic but I'll be there soon."

"Am I a joke to you?"

"What's that?"

"Am…I…a joke to you? One of your little bitches on the side?"

"No Shereece not at all I-"

"If you're not here in fifteen minutes, turn your car back around." Shereece then cut off the phone.

"He'll be here soon," Shereece said to Kia while sitting next to her open coffin.

"Come here Ricky, crawl to me." Ricky crawled over to Shereece wearing only the black leather mask with the zip as the mouth piece. Ricky peered over at the coffin getting a good look at Kia. Kia stared at Ricky. It had been a while since she had seen Ricky for the first time, so she stared deep.

Shereece started rubbing Ricky on his leather covered head like he was a puppy.

"Say hello again to Ricky Kia, a truly devoted slave of mine. He's going to be joining us for our ceremony this evening. You see Kia, if you're in my cult you must be there whenever a human sacrifice is taking place. I want to fully introduce you two now." Kia unzipped Ricky's mouth piece.

"It's ok Ricky. Say hello. She's going to be a new member of our cult real soon," said Shereece.

"Hello Kia," said Ricky.

"Hello Ricky. Why do you have on that mask?" Kia asked curiously.

"I like it, and my Mistress likes it," replied Ricky.

"Yes I do," said Shereece as she looked down at Ricky.

"Take off your mask. I want to see you without your mask on," said Kia.

Ricky looked at Shereece to seek her approval. Shereece took Ricky's mask off, exposing his face for Kia to see. Kia stared at Ricky's face.

"That's better. So how long have you been my sister's slave Ricky?" Just as Kia asked that question, Shereece's phone started ringing. It was Freddy. After two rings Shereece picked up the phone.

"Where are you?" Shereece asked straight away.

"I'm outside your house."

"Give me a minute, I'm coming to the door," said Shereece before hanging up.

"Right, he's here!" Shereece said sternly. "Are you sure you're ready for this Kia?"

"Yes I'm ready."

"You better be. Ricky, get in your position." Shereece ordered as she clicked her fingers and pointed at the lit candles.

Ricky crawled away and placed himself behind the circle of candles with a pentagram in the middle that Shereece had prepared.

"I'll be back soon, said Shereece to Kia before kissing her two fingers and pressing them on Kia's lips. She closed Kia's coffin lid and headed out of the basement then walked to her front door.

"What time do you call this?" said Shereece after opening her front door to Freddy.

"I'm sorry honey, I think there was a car accident or something because the traffic was terrible."

"Save your excuses. You're lucky you made it within the fifteen minutes or I would have blocked your arse."

Freddy smiled. "Are those for me?" asked Shereece, looking at the bunch of red velvet flowers in a wrap that Freddy was holding in his right hand.

"Yes Shereece, I believe these are for you." Freddy handed the flowers to Shereece, then he leaned in towards her and attempted to kiss her on the lips, but Shereece turned her face and Freddy's kiss landed on her cheek. Freddy smiled and leaned back, then looked Shereece up and down.

Shereece was wearing a black one shoulder split bodycon dress. Her toned right thigh could be seen through the split. Freddy was looking at her thigh with lustful admiration.

"You look spectacular," said Freddy. Shereece smiled and moved to her left, indicating for Freddy to enter her house.

Freddy walked in. He was wearing a black suit along with a pair of black suede Gucci shoes, with a white long sleeve shirt underneath his blazer.

"I like your suit," Shereece complimented.

"How could you not? It's Armani," said Freddy with his back to her.

"Still cocky I see." Freddy turned around to face Shereece and smiled at her.

"Let me get that," said Shereece, referring to Freddy's blazer. She removed Freddy's blazer and hung it up on the end of her banister.

"Take your shoes off," said Shereece. Freddy took his size 11 shoes off, and Shereece took them and placed them under her staircase.

"Follow me," said Shereece as she walked through her long corridor. The corridor lights were on and Freddy looked around. They got to the living room. The living room lights were also on. Freddy looked up to the living room ceiling to get a good look at Shereece's sparkling crystal chandelier which she had recently bought. He then looked around Shereece's living room.

"This is a nice place you've got here."

"I know it is."

"Oh, now who's being cocky?" Shereece giggled and pushed Freddy down onto her long leather sofa. She picked up her TV remote control from her dining table and turned her 57inch plasma TV.

"Here, make yourself at home," said Shereece as she threw the remote to Freddy. Freddy caught the remote.

What are you having to drink?" asked Shereece.

"What have you got?"

"Courvoisier, E & J, Malibu."

"I'll have a glass of Malibu. Do you have any mixers to go with that?"

"Pineapple juice or coke."

"Pineapple juice."

"Cool. Make yourself comfortable. I'll be back in two ticks."

"I'll see you in two ticks." Shereece went into her kitchen, took the Malibu out of her cupboard along with two medium size drinking glasses. She filled up Freddy's glass with Malibu and pineapple juice, then she delved into her purse and took out the Rohypnol. She mixed the drug into the glass of Malibu she prepared for Freddy. She then went into her fridge and took out a small bottle of Coke and poured herself a glass before returning the bottle to the fridge. She returned to the living room and handed Freddy his glass.

"Thank you," said Freddy as he took the glass while barely taking his eyes off the TV screen. "I love this movie," said Freddy.

"What movie is it?"

"Halloween."

"Halloween?" Shereece repeated in indication that she didn't know the movie.

"Yeah, you know, Halloween, Michael Myers." Shereece had a bewildered expression on her face.

"Wow, it's a classic. I take it you're not into horrors," said Freddy.

"No, I'm not into horrors. I prefer romantic movies," said Shereece as she sat on her sofa opposite Freddy.

"Oh yeah? What's your favourite romance movie then?" Freddy asked whilst looking at Shereece.

"Pretty Woman," Shereece replied.

"Ahhh what, with Richard Gere, and how he falls in love with a prostitute," said Freddy before laughing. "I'd never date a hooker."

Given her profession as a dominatrix, it burned Shereece hearing how Freddy spoke about dating a prostitute.

"What's wrong with dating a prostitute?" asked Shereece.

"Are you serious? What's right with it? They're dirty, aren't they? Having sex with multiple men for money. How can anybody take a woman like that seriously?"

"Well why can't someone take a woman like that seriously? A prostitute is just a business woman. Business is supply and demand, and sex happens to be in high demand. They're just supplying a lucrative service. You can't knock that."

"They're dirty though. They have no respect for themselves. The body is a temple of God. It shouldn't be sold for sex," said Freddy passionately.

"Don't give me that body is a temple shit. If I opened up my legs to you, you'd fuck me right now."

"Ahh but I wouldn't pay for it," said Freddy making a point.

"Yes you would. Taking a woman out for meals, paying for dinners in hopes of getting some pussy at the end of the night, it's technically the same thing."

"Nah it's different." Freddy continued speaking but Shereece tuned out of the conversation. She couldn't hear a word Freddy was saying anymore. She stared at Freddy with her eyes narrowed and imagined stabbing him multiple times in his chest. There was a long pause before Shereece snapped out of her fantasy and caught the end of Freddy's sentence which was, "you understand?"

"Sorry?" said Shereece as she shook her head.

"Do you understand what I'm saying?"

"Oh yeah, yeah I hear you," said Shereece pretending to know what he was talking about. She then looked at Freddy's glass and could see it was nearly full. "You know you've barely touched your drink. Are you a light drinker or something?"

"Oh no not all, I just like to slowly sip my drinks. There's no rush. What are you drinking by the way? I can see it's not Malibu."

"E & J and coke," Shereece lied.

"Ok. So Shereece, about last time-"

"Let's not talk about that. It was a bad night. I was being a bit of a bitch."

"No. Well let's not put it all on you."

"Really, let's not talk about it. Tonight's a new night. I've invited you to my place, so I must like something about you."

"Yeah you're right. Let's not talk about it," said Freddy giving in. I'm glad to hear you like something about me. Let's toast, to a new start," Freddy insisted as he held his drink up. Shereece also raised her drink and Freddy stepped over and touched his glass on hers. After doing that, he took a big gulp of his drink."

"Oh wow, that was a big sip for someone who says they like to drink slowly."

"Well not after a toast." Freddy and Shereece shared a giggle, before Freddy sat back down on the sofa. Shereece picked up her TV remote and started flicking through channels.

"Hey what's going on? I was watching that," said Freddy not sounding too serious.

"Would you rather watch that or would you rather watch me?"

"Oh I'd rather watch you baby."

"Good." She turned off her TV and put down the remote on her dining table.

"So, how are your twins?"

"They're good, they're good. They're in bed right now. How's your daughter?"

"She's good. She's at her mother's. I'm picking her up tomorrow."

"Oh that's nice."

"She's beautiful, my daughter. Truly the love of my life. Want to see her?" Freddy offered.

"Yeah sure." Freddy took a sip of his drink before pulling out his iPhone 11 and getting up to sit beside Shereece. He went into his phone and started to scroll through his picture gallery before stopping on a picture of a beautiful young black girl with her hair plaited into tiny cornrows. She was sitting on a park swing smiling.

"That's my little girl right there," Freddy said while pointing at the picture of his daughter.

"Wow. She's really beautiful," said Shereece.

"She takes after her Dad," replied Freddy arrogantly as he looked at Shereece's face smiling. Shereece and Freddy were now making eye contact. Their faces were inches away from each other.

"I've got a surprise for you Mr Confident," Shereece whispered.

"Oh yeah. What surprise is that?" Shereece stood up.

"Take off all your clothes," said Shereece boldly.

"Take off all my clothes?" repeated Freddy.

"Yes, everything."

"Ok," said Freddy with a big grin on his face. Freddy started stripping off, excited about the surprise Shereece was going to give him.

"I'll be back," said Shereece as she left the living room and went up to her bedroom. Ten minutes later she returned to her living room naked with a bottle of baby oil. Freddy was now fully naked lying on the sofa. He had finished his glass of Malibu. Freddy looked at Shereece and sat upright. Shereece walked up to him and held his jaw with her right hand.

"Are you ready for your surprise?" asked Shereece seductively.

"Yes Shereece, I'm ready."

"Nah, I don't think you are. Turn around and lie on your stomach." Freddy did what he was told. Shereece opened the bottle of baby oil and poured some of it down Freddy's back.

"Eww, it's cold," said Freddy as he shook a little.

"Just relax." Shereece knew by relaxing Freddy, the drug she spiked him with would take effect quicker. She kneeled down on the floor beside the sofa, and started giving Freddy an intense back massage.

"Oh, I like this surprise," Freddy mumbled.

"This isn't your surprise," replied Shereece. Shereece's words echoed in Freddy's ears. It was as if she was talking under water.

"You know what, I think I've had too much to drink," said Freddy as he struggled to turn his head to look at her.

"How can you have had too much? You've only had one glass," said Shereece smiling. Freddy was now seeing double of Shereece.

"Yeah I know, but then, why am I feeling like this?"

"Feeling like what?" Freddy attempted to get up right before Shereece put him in a chokehold and dragged him off the sofa.

"Now you're going to see your surprise," Shereece whispered in his ear. Freddy was defenceless. The drug had crept up on him. Shereece pulled him towards the basement trap door, opened it, then pulled Freddy by the neck down the stairs with her after closing the trap door.

When she got to the bottom of the steps she lifted up Freddy with both her arms in a cradle position and carried him over to the pentagram, carefully stepping over the lit candles to lay him on his back. Ricky was still behind the candles kneeling on the floor obediently.

Freddy started to try and talk. Barely conscious, he mumbled the words, "Where am I? What's going on?"

Shereece bent down and put her face over Freddy's, and whispered the words, "You're in hell Freddy, and I'm the devil," then she burst out laughing.

"You ok Ricky?"

"Yes Mistress Lilith."

"Are you ready for the party?"

"Yes Mistress Lilith." Shereece stood up and walked over to Kia's coffin. She unlocked it then lifted up the lid. Kia looked up at Shereece's naked body.

"Are you ready Kia? Your human sacrifice awaits you." Kia took a deep breath, closed her eyes then opened them again.

"I'm ready," said Kia. Shereece smiled and lifted Kia up off of her back. She went into her purse and took out the key to unlock Kia's shackled ankles. She then helped Kia to stand up. After being shackled for so long she was unsteady on her feet.

"Come with me," said Shereece. She walked Kia over to Freddy's helpless body. Kia looked down at Freddy. Shereece went into her bag and brought out her Rambo knife and held it out to Kia.

"This is it Kia, your ticket to freedom. Join us. Slay him and join us. Give your soul to Satan! You will see the miracles he works for you," said Shereece passionately. Kia took the knife from Shereece.

"Uncuff me," said Kia. Shereece put her hand in her purse and took out her handgun, then cocked it back before saying, "Can I trust you?"

"Stop hesitating and let's do this shit!" Kia said sternly. Shereece smiled then took Kia by the wrists, unlocked the handcuffs, and took them off. Kia started to wiggle her wrists and hands around. Shereece took a step to the side making sure she had a good view of Kia and Freddy.

She then took her iPhone out of her bag and went to the video option. Kia sat on top of Freddy's stomach and lifted the knife up in the air with both hands. Kia looked over the faces of Shereece and Ricky before looking back down to Freddy's face. Freddy squinted his eyes up at Kia before slowly saying, "Who....the....fuck....are....you?"

"I don't know you, but this has to be done!" replied Kia. Then she plunged the knife into the left side of Freddy's chest, piercing his heart.

Freddy's eyes and mouth opened wide in shock and pain. Kia pulled the knife out and stabbed him again, and again. She kept on repeatably stabbing him in the chest and neck.

Shereece was recording the whole scene. All of Kia's anger and rage from being held captive for so long, and the death of her husband was all coming out through her stabbing frenzy. Blood was squirting out of Freddy's chest and neck as Kia stabbed him, and Kia's face and hands were covered in his blood.

In total she stabbed him a multiple of fifteen times. She finally stopped when she saw Freddy's eyes roll to the back of his head. She was breathing heavily, then burst into tears. Shereece stopped recording. She then knelt down beside Kia and put her right arm around her shoulders.

"Don't worry babe, you did it. You're one of us now." Kia looked into Shereece's face, dropped the knife on the floor and hugged Shereece tightly. Shereece returned Kia's hug, kissed her on the cheek softly, then on her mouth.

"You did well babe, you did great....There's just one more thing we have to do." Shereece picked the knife up from the floor.

"Move aside sis."

Kia got off of Freddy's corpse. Shereece then plunged the knife into Freddy's already butchered chest and sliced deeper into it, reached her hand in and ripped his heart out.

Holding Freddy's heart high up in the air, she looked at Kia and said, loudly, "Repeat these words!" She then held Freddy's heart over Kia's head and sliced it open.

"Hail Satan! Hail Satan!" Shereece chanted as the blood oozed over Kia's head and face.

"Hail Satan! Hail Satan!" Ricky chanted.

"Hail Satan! Hail Satan! Hail Satan!" Kia shouted at the top of her lungs simultaneously bashing her right fist in the air.

Shereece squeezed the heart over Ricky's head while he was chanting, then over her own.

"Hail Satan! Hail Satan! Yes dad, we have her now! We have her now!" Shereece screamed at the top of her lungs. Kia stopped chanting.

"What? what did you just say?" Kia asked baffled. Just as she asked that question, the wall at the far end of the basement in front of Kia and Shereece started to open.

Ricky turned around to face the opening wall. A bright white light from the open wall shone through the basement. Kia and Shereece's father Mark Corret emerged from behind the wall in a wheelchair.

He rolled his wheelchair over to the three of them. Shereece threw her arms around him and hugged him tightly. He looked old and wrinkly with a completely bald head but had a thick, long, grey beard and a moustache. Despite his aged looks, Kia still recognised him.

"Dad?" said Kia. Shereece kissed her dad on his lips. He embraced her kiss. Then he looked down at Kia.

"You see Kia, I never left you," said Mark.

"Dad is a submissive. He trained me since we were teenagers how to be his dom. All from this basement. He taught me all about sadism and satanic worship. We kept it secret from you for years. He became a recluse, and after building the secret room he just came out of, he has never left this basement," Shereece told Kia.

"I see everything from there, everything I desire to see," said Mark.

"What do you mean?" asked Kia looking bewildered. Shereece held her hand out to Kia and said, "Come with me." Kia hesitated.

"Don't be afraid Kia. Come with me." Kia reached her hand out to Shereece who took Kia's hand and lifted her up. She kissed Mark on his head and said, "I'll be right back Dad."

She walked Kia into the secret room. The room was large. The walls were red. There were three 47-inch monitor screens on one of the walls with a black desk inches from the wall which held a computer keyboard with a microphone connected to it. On the middle monitor screen you could see the basement.

"Dad can see the whole house from this room through these three screens. There are cameras planted all over this house, but most importantly in this basement. This here is what he likes to watch," said Shereece pointing at the middle monitor.

"He watches me dominate subs in here and make human sacrifices while he masturbates." Kia looked at Shereece's face and then closed her eyes for two seconds trying to take in all of the disturbing revelations, then opened them again still reeling. Mark rolled his wheelchair into the room.

"Mum was into this too before she died," said Shereece.

"So why now? Why show and tell me all this now?" asked Kia in anger.

"Because we needed you to kill first in order to trust you. At first, we weren't even going to recruit you. But I wanted a child. As you already know I can't conceive. So, I went into nursery work to be closer to kids. But that wasn't good enough. I needed to raise a child as my own. And for a while, I thought I had found my perfect child - April, an infant at my nursery."

"You, you kidnapped missing April?" asked Kia surprised and shocked.

"Yes, yes I did. It didn't work out though, so I killed her. I took her life. She's in one of the coffins right now," said Shereece without showing any remorse.

"How could you Shereece?! How could you kill a child?!" shouted Kia.

"Lower your tone Kia. It had to be that way. I enjoy killing, but April was unfortunate. I wanted her but she refused me. She wanted her real mother. After that incident, I knew I needed to raise a child from birth in order to have full loyalty."

"Why didn't you just adopt?"

"No. I wanted it to be my own flesh and blood. I wanted it from you. I was actually going to kill you after you had the babies, but it was dad's idea to keep you alive and for you to join us."

"You're my flesh and blood, I couldn't let you die," Mark inserted himself into the conversation.

"What about that letter?" asked Kia.

"What letter?" replied Mark.

"The note you left me and Shereece fourteen years ago, blaming me for mum's death, calling me a devil bitch."

"Oh, that note. It was part of mine and Shereece's plan. Shereece had always been my special one out of the two of you.

After I decided I was never going to leave this house again, I told Shereece, but couldn't tell you because I knew you wouldn't understand.

I knew you wouldn't be involved in my fetishes. So, you see, I had to leave you a letter so you would think I left you. I made it brutal on your behalf so you wouldn't come looking for me, after all, why would you want to find a father who hates you?"

"So you've been grooming Shereece all her life?" said Kia in disgust.

"I wouldn't call it grooming Kia, but to answer your question, from the age of twelve and upwards I've been teaching Shereece about submissives and dominants. It was our little secret. It wasn't until she was fourteen I started teaching her about satanism. It's nothing to be ashamed of Kia. It runs in your blood. My father was into satanism and so was his father before that and your mother. Anyway, we're one big happy family now," said Mark as he put his arm around Shereece's waist and smiled. They both stared at Kia. Kia felt ready to vomit but held it back.

"Why the wheelchair?" asked Kia.

"Not long after you left the house, daddy had a stroke. I've been taking care of him ever since," replied Shereece.

"Ok, so what now? I've made my sacrifice, just like you wanted. What now?" asked Kia.

"Well now we all get clean of course, we're covered in blood," Shereece said laughing.

"You know what I mean. I'm free now right? Free from this basement?" Kia asked.

"I keep my promises Kia. It's in dad's will. Yes you're free now. You can live back in your room, and we'll take care of the babies and dad together. That's understood right?" Shereece clarified.

"Yes, that's understood. I'm fine with that," replied Kia relieved to hear she was free from her coffin even if not free from Shereece.

"Alright, you two both go and get clean," said Mark.

"Come on Kia," said Shereece as she extended her arm out to Kia's. Kia took Shereece's offered hand and they walked out of their father's room. As they walked past Ricky, Kia asked, "What about him?"

"Get rid of him. He's a liability Shereece. We have Kia in our cult now. The three of us is enough," said Mark.

"But I like having my servant dad. He's been so obedient to me. He's a good servant."

"I forbid it. I only suggested you bring slaves into this cult because I didn't know if Kia would come along. Now Kia is with us, he must go," said Mark sternly. Ricky started shaking in fear. Shereece raised her gun to Ricky's forehead.

"Oh fuck, please don't Shereece please, please, I've done nothing wrong," said Ricky shaking his head.

"I know Ricky baby, but my dad is right. You're wanted but not needed, and that could be a problem."

"You can't kill one of your own!" Ricky cried out.

"You're not family Ricky. Only blood family is my own now." BANG! Shereece shot Ricky right between the eyes. Ricky's body slumped to the floor. After all the ordeal Kia went through, she wasn't fazed by Ricky's murder.

"Come Kia," said Shereece. The girls walked towards the basement stairs.

"You'll make a great dominatrix Kia!" Mark shouted out from across the basement. Kia and Shereece stopped walking and looked back at their father.

"I'll be back soon dad," said Shereece, then turned back to lead Kia up the stairs.

As Shereece reached the top of the stairs, she unlocked the trap door and looked behind her at Kia.

"It's been a long while since you've been out of here Kia. Are you ready to step out?"

"Yes, I'm ready." Shereece opened the trapdoor and as she emerged she was met by Detective Crease and Detective Mary standing in the middle of her living room. The living room lights were on.

"Freeze! Come out with both your hands behind your head!" Detective Crease shouted. Shereece did as Detective Crease asked. Both detectives' eyes opened wide when they saw Shereece's naked body covered in blood.

"Who else is down there?!" asked Detective Mary.

"Go see for yourself," replied Shereece smiling.

"If anybody else is down there come out with your hands in the air!" Detective Crease shouted.

"I'm coming up!" shouted Kia. Kia came out of the basement with her hands in the air.

"Who are you?" Detective Mary asked Kia, taking in Kia's pale face along with the red marks on her wrists and ankles and her blood-soaked pink nightie.

Kia was a far cry from looking like her usual self. Her extensions had been removed by Shereece and her own hair was a mess with many grey strands. Her yoga toned body had disappeared after being trapped for over a year in a box. She looked frail and terrified.

"Keep quiet. I know our rights. Don't say anything," said Shereece to Kia. Kia looked at Shereece then looked back at the detectives without saying a word.

"Why are you both covered in blood? What have you done?" demanded Detective Crease. Shereece stayed silent.

"You've been on surveillance Shereece. That's right. We've been watching your house all day. We know you kidnap and possibly kill people. We kicked in your door when we heard a gunshot. We've radioed in for back up. Armed police are already on their way. Where are the two men who entered your property today? Did you kill them?!" said Detective Crease loudly.

"Shereece, you and whoever you are under arrest for suspicion of kidnap and murder. You do not have to say anything, but it may harm your defence if you do not mention when questioned, something you later rely on in court. Anything you do or say maybe given in evidence,"

Detective Crease read them their rights. He then took out a set of handcuffs from his waist, then approached Shereece with them. As he took a step towards her, Shereece gripped Detective Crease by the throat. Detective Crease grabbed Shereece by the wrists and tried to loosen her grip.

Detective Mary jumped on Shereece's back and tried to pull her off of Detective Crease. Kia in all the commotion ran out of the living room and up the stairs. All she could think about was her babies. She started going into all the bedrooms until she found the one with Shyla and Peree.

She picked the sleeping babies up from the cot they were in then all of a sudden, BANG! BANG! BANG! She heard three gunshots from downstairs. She held the babies tight to her chest and started sobbing.

"Please God, let me and my babies get out of this in one piece," Kia said to herself. She ran out the room and down the stairs until she bumped into Shereece halfway down. Both now standing in the middle of the stairs, Shereece had her right hand gripped on her Beretta handgun.

"Going somewhere without me Kia?" Shereece asked sarcastically.

"I had to make sure the babies were ok," Kia responded fearfully trying to hold the babies tight. Shereece looked at the babies in Kia's trembling arms then looked into Kia's eyes.

"Those two detectives are dead. I killed them both. Now we have to move quick. More police will be on their way."

"Where we going to go?" Kia asked in panic.

"Come with me." said Shereece before she turned around and ran down the stairs. When she got to the bottom of the stairs, she turned around and realised that Kia was still standing in the middle of the stairs. Kia's legs were shaking. "Kia what are you doing?"

"But where are we going?" Kia asked in confusion and paralysed with fear.

"Kia come the fuck on!" Shereece shouted aggressively. Kia snapped out of it and realising she had no choice, she walked down the stairs quickly. Shereece walked to the front door and saw the hinges had been kicked off.

"Shit!" exclaimed Shereece. She then peeped outside and couldn't see anybody in sight. "We've still got time. Come on."

She walked swiftly through her corridor and into her living room. Kia followed behind her. The thought of dashing through the front door and out the house crossed Kia's mind but she didn't act on it, fearing that Shereece would shoot her in the back.

Shereece stepped over the dead bodies of Detective Crease and Detective Mary. Kia looked at the bodies realising her hopes of being saved by police were gone. She thought about her murdering Freddy and how Shereece had video recorded the whole thing.

She turned her face away from the dead detectives not liking the sight. Shereece went to the basement trap door, unlocked it and lifted it open. "Why are we going back down there Shereece?" Kia asked with growing confusion.

"We need to get dad," Shereece emphasised.

"Shereece come on let's go, there's no time for that. The police are on their way," said Kia.

"We're not going anywhere without dad. Now come on!" Shereece demanded.

Kia stalled.

"I said come on Kia!" Shereece repeated fiercely and pointed her gun at Kia. Kia looked at the gun then proceeded to go down the basement steps, holding the babies carefully. The babies woke up and started crying.

Shereece went down the steps behind Kia after closing the basement trap door. When they got to the bottom of the stairs, Shereece ran over to her father who was sitting in his wheelchair in the camera room with the wall still open. She hugged him and broke down in tears.

"It's over now daddy. They're coming for us," said Shereece as she held on to her father.

"It's ok darling. I saw everything on camera. It's ok, it's ok. You know what we've got to do now," said Mark while rubbing the side of Shereece's head.

"Yes daddy, I know what we've got to do. Kia come here." Kia couldn't hear much over the babies crying. Shereece reached out her arm to beckon Kia over to her. Kia walked over to Shereece and her dad, passing the corpses of Freddy and Ricky. Mark looked at his monitor that captured the living room and could see armed police had swarmed it. The police officers could see a blood trail that led to the basement trap door.

"Get the petrol. We haven't got much time," said Mark to Shereece.

"Petrol?" asked Kia hoping she heard wrong. Shereece ran to the corner of the basement and emerged seconds later with a green fuel can that contained petrol.

"The ultimate sacrifice to Satan Kia, is our own lives," said Mark. Shereece then doused Kia and the babies with petrol before Kia had fully taken in what her father had said.

"No! You're crazy! I'm getting the fuck out of here now!" screamed Kia.

"You try and leave us and I'll shoot you. You won't make it to the staircase. Don't make me do that. This is the best way to go Kia. We'll dwell in Satan's kingdom as queens. Or do you want to spend the rest of your life in prison? It's all on camera Kia. You murdering Freddy, all of my killings. We'll be sent to prison forever."

"You lied to me. What happened to Satan never allowing you to get caught huh? What happened to that?" shouted Kia.

"It all makes sense now Kia. We're not caught if we sacrifice ourselves. Me and dad agreed if a day like this should come, we'll sacrifice ourselves in a ball of flames to Satan."

"You have to believe Kia. Perish with us on earth and live forever in hell as Satan's angels!" said Mark.

"Come out! Come out now! We know you're down there, we can hear you! Get the fuck out here now or we're coming down! We're armed and we will shoot!" shouted an armed police officer from upstairs.

Shereece doused herself with petrol, then doused Mark. She picked up one of the lit candles from the floor.

"Kia trust me, this is the best way. Have faith in this thing of ours," said Shereece. Kia thought about prison and knew she wouldn't survive a day in there.

"But what about the babies?" cried Kia desperately.

"We'll raise them in Satan's kingdom," replied Shereece. "Are we all ready?!" Shereece shouted.

"Yes I'm ready!" said Mark as he nodded his head. Kia closed her eyes with tears rolling down her cheeks.

"When you're in flames Kia, make sure you repeat the words 'Hail Satan'," Shereece said, then she put the candle's flame on her father. He went up in flames and yelled, "Hail Satan" as he burned.

Kia opened her eyes and immediately tried to run to the basement stairs.

"Where the fuck are you going?!" screamed Shereece before chasing Kia. She grabbed Kia's nightie and put the lit candle to Kia's waist. Kia started to go up in flames. In a desperate attempt to try and save her babies Kia threw them on the floor before they could catch fire. Shereece tried to go after the babies to set them alight but Kia grabbed Shereece in a tight hug before she could get to them.

Shereece's body lit up in flames from Kia's burning body. They both fell to the floor in flames. Shereece grabbed Kia's head and turned her her face to hers. She began laughing hysterically before screaming, "I'll see you in hell Kia! Hail Satan."

Kia passed out and soon died. One of the armed police officers forced the basement trap door open with a sledge hammer, then a swarm of officers descended the basement stairs.

"Oh my God," said the first armed officer down the stairs as he saw all three bodies burning and Shyla and Peree crying on the floor.

THE END

You can find out more about the
author on social media:

Instagram: @twininacoffin
Twitter: @DeanEkaragha
Facebook: Dean Ekaragha
Instagram: @DeanEkaragha

Printed in Great Britain
by Amazon

80613648R00120